STORY TIME

Written by Philippa Wingate
and Matthew Morgan
Edited by Philippa Wingate
Designed by Zoe Quayle
Illustrations by Caroline Anstey, Penny Ives,
Robin Lawrie and Martin Ursell
Production by Joanne Rooke
Reproduction by Colourwise Limited

First published in Great Britain in 2002 by Buster Books,
an imprint of Michael O'Mara Books Limited,
9 Lion Yard, Tremadoc Road, London, SW4 7NQ

Story Time copyright © 2002 Buster Books

A CIP catalogue record for this book is available
from the British Library

ISBN 1–903840–36–8

3 5 7 9 10 8 6 4 2

Visit our website at www.mombooks.com

Printed in China by WKT Company Limited

STORY TIME

Buster
Books

CONTENTS

10 minutes

15 minutes

The Pied Piper of Hamelin

A fat, black rat with razor-sharp teeth and a trailing tail stared out of the cupboard at the cook.

"RAAAAAAT!" she screeched, and jumped up on to a chair.

At first only a few rats were spotted in the town of Hamelin. Then there were a hundred rats, then a thousand, then ten thousand rats. Eventually there were a million rats.

The townsfolk chased them out of their houses, threw water over them and baited traps with poisoned cheese. But the rats wouldn't go away.

In desperation, the people gathered outside the mayor's house in the main square.

"Help us get rid of the rats," they shouted. "What are you going to do?"

"Um... er... well, er... I'm thinking about it," mumbled the mayor, who didn't have a clue what to do.

"I can help," said a strong, confident voice.

The crowd parted, and a stranger walked towards the mayor. His tunic was a vivid green, he wore a bright red and yellow cloak, and he had a feather tucked into his hat. In his hand he carried a golden pipe. He was the Pied Piper.

"I can get rid of the rats," said the man. "But you will have to pay me a million pieces of gold."

"That's an awful lot of money," groaned the mayor.

"There are an awful lot of rats," smiled the stranger.

"It's a deal. When can you start?" asked the mayor, and the people began to cheer.

"By morning there won't be a rat left in Hamelin," promised the Pied Piper.

As the sun set, the piper began to play. His music floated across the square, into every street and every doorway. Then something moved in a dark alley. A fat, black rat pricked up its ears. Then another rat listened, and another. As the piper played, rats began to flood into the streets. They followed him as he danced toward the town gates. When the piper came to the river, he waded in until the water reached his middle. The rats swarmed after him, drowning in the icy water.

Next morning, the Pied Piper knocked at the doors of the mayor's house.

"The rats have gone," he said. "One million pieces of gold, please."

"Nonsense, I can't possibly pay you all that money," grumbled the mayor.

"Are you breaking your promise?" asked the piper, narrowing his eyes and baring his little teeth. "You will regret this." And with that, he vanished.
The mayor breathed a sigh of relief.

"What a brilliant man I am. I have saved Hamelin from the rats, completely free of charge!"

The mayor slept soundly that night and so did everyone else in the town – except for the children.

In the middle of the night, they awoke to hear a haunting tune drifting through their bedroom windows. First one child ran into the square. Then another skipped past, and another. Soon every child in Hamelin was gathered in the main square. The Pied Piper turned and danced toward the city gates. The children followed him.

Outside the city, they crossed the bridge and danced through the forest until they reached a great mountain. As the piper played, a vast rock in the cliff-face began to move. It slid aside, revealing a huge cave. In danced the children, following the piper. Behind them the rock slid back, sealing the mouth of the cave.

The children of Hamelin were never seen again. Only a lame boy who had not been able to keep up with the others was found outside the cave. He told the townsfolk what had happened. They searched day and night for a year, but they never found a way into the cave. Occasionally, some mothers thought they could hear the eerie notes of a golden pipe, but the Pied Piper never returned to Hamelin.

The Ugly Duckling

Once upon a time, in a farmyard far away, lived Mother Duck. Seven shiny new eggs lay in her nest and she sat on them patiently.

One sunny morning the eggs began to hatch. One... two... three... four... five... six.... Out popped six fluffy, yellow ducklings. But the seventh egg was bigger than the others, and it didn't hatch. Mother Duck couldn't even remember laying seven eggs. She only remembered laying six. How had it got there?

Tap, tap! Someone was pecking inside the egg, trying to get out. Sure enough, out popped a strange-looking duckling. He had brown feathers, not yellow feathers like his brothers and sisters.

"I can't understand how this ugly duckling can be one of my babies!" Mother Duck thought.

Well, the ugly duckling may not have been pretty, but he was certainly hungry. He ate twice as much as his brothers and sisters, and grew bigger and bigger. Soon they didn't want to play with him because he was so clumsy. The ugly duckling felt sad and lonely.

"Nobody loves me. Why am I so different?"

One day, he decided to run away. When he reached a pond, he saw some ducks swimming by.

"Do you know of any ducklings with feathers like mine?" he asked. They shook their heads.

"We don't know anyone as ugly as you," they laughed spitefully.

On he went until he came to a cottage. The old woman who lived there caught the duckling by his tail.

"I'll keep this goose, and maybe it will lay lots of eggs for my dinner," said the old woman.

Her eyesight was so bad that she couldn't tell the ugly duckling was a boy duckling, and would never lay any eggs. In fact, the old woman's eyesight was so bad she couldn't even see that the duckling wasn't a goose at all.

For weeks the duckling sat in the old woman's barn.

"If you don't lay eggs soon, the old woman will pop you in her pot," warned the cat who lived in the cottage. The old woman kept stuffing the duckling with food.

"If you won't lay eggs, hurry up and get plump so I can eat you for my dinner," she threatened.
The ugly duckling was so scared he lost his appetite.

"All I wanted was to find someone who would love me," he cried.

One night, finding the door of the barn open, the duckling escaped. He waddled away from the cottage as fast as his webbed feet would carry him. By morning he found himself in a bed of reeds.

"Nobody wants me," the ugly duckling wept. "I think I'll just hide here."

Winter came and the water in the bed of reeds froze. The ground became so thickly covered with snow that the duckling couldn't find any food. One day he sank to the ground, hungry and exhausted. At that moment a friendly farmer was passing by. He picked up the duckling and popped him into the pocket of his coat.

"Poor little thing, you're frozen," said the farmer. "I'll take you home. My children will look after you."

The farmer's children loved the ugly duckling and took great care of him. He was very happy. When spring came, however, he had grown so big that the farmer decided it was time to take him back to the pond.

As the duckling looked down into the pond he saw his own reflection in the water.

"Goodness!" he cried. "How I've changed. I am big and white and…"

"…and beautiful," said a group of swans gliding past. "You are a handsome swan, just like us."
A group of children who were playing on the riverbank pointed at him.

"Look at that young swan. He's the finest of them all," they shouted.

And his heart almost burst with happiness.

13

The Emperor with Goat's Ears

Once upon a time, there was a great and powerful emperor, but unlike any other emperor, he had ears like a goat. Of course he was very embarrassed about his large, hairy ears. Every morning, a barber came to the palace to shave the emperor, and every morning the emperor questioned the barber.

"Do you notice anything strange about me?" he asked. Nervously, each barber always replied, "Sir, you have goat's ears." Sadly, each barber was always put to death.

Eventually there were no more barbers left in the city. The Master of the Company of Barbers called one of his apprentices.

"Peter, you must go and shave the emperor," he said.

When he arrived at the palace, Peter was taken to the emperor's bedroom. Carefully he began to spread lather on the emperor's chin.

"Boy, do you notice anything strange about me?" asked the emperor.

"Nothing, Sir," replied Peter.
The emperor was delighted. He gave Peter twelve pieces of gold and said, "You must come every day to shave me." Every morning Peter went to shave the emperor and was paid twelve pieces of gold. Everything seemed wonderful, but the secret of the emperor's ears began to bother Peter.

14

It was like a pain in his tummy. He longed to tell somebody.

The Master of the Company of Barbers noticed that Peter had something on his mind.

"What is troubling you, Peter?" he asked.

"I know something nobody else knows, but I can never tell anyone," admitted Peter.

The Master was a wise man and suggested, "Go to a field outside the city. Dig a hole and whisper your secret three times into the hole. Then put all the earth back into the hole and come home. You will feel much better."

Peter did as he was told. He dug a hole.

"The emperor has goat's ears," he whispered three times. Straightaway he felt better. Carefully he put the earth back into the hole and skipped home.

Soon an elder tree began to grow in the hole. One day some shepherds noticed the tree. One of them cut a stem from it to make a flute. But when the shepherd lifted the flute to his lips and began to play, not a note came out. Instead the flute sang, "The emperor has goat's ears."

Before long the whole town had heard of the magical flute and what it had sung. When the news reached the emperor, he sent for Peter immediately.

"What have you told people about me?" demanded the emperor.

"Nothing, your Majesty," Peter swore. But the emperor didn't believe him and drew his sword. Terrified, Peter immediately confessed what he had done.

"Fetch my chariot," ordered the emperor. The emperor and Peter rode out of the city, followed by all the courtiers.

When they reached the place where the elder grew, they found only one stem left on the tree. The emperor ordered a servant to cut it down and make a flute. Then he ordered his chamberlain to play it. As the chamberlain blew, the flute sang, "The emperor has goat's ears."

Peter shook with fear. The emperor thought for a moment.

"I will spare your life because you didn't tell a living person my secret," he decided. "You told the earth and the earth gave away the secret. However, I don't think I want you to be my barber anymore."

Peter left the city and become a barber in another country, just in case the emperor changed his mind.

17

The Three Little Pigs

Once upon a time, there were three little pigs who lived in a beautiful green valley. Each pig had a house. The first had a house made from straw. The second pig had a house made from wood, and the third pig had a house made from bricks. The pigs loved their houses and each of them secretly thought that their house was the best house. All in all, they were three very happy little pigs. But not for long.

One day a hairy, old wolf came sniffling and snuffling through the valley. He was a mean and cunning wolf, a greedy and sly wolf, but most of all he was a hungry old wolf.

"Yum, yum," the wolf thought to himself. "Three juicy little piggies for my supper."
He prowled around the houses working out how to get in, and it wasn't long before he had a plan.

The first pig was sitting in his straw house reading a book when the wolf knocked at the door.

"Little pig, little pig, let me come in," said the wolf. The pig thought a moment about opening the door, but he had been told about wolves and how dangerous they could be.

"No, I won't," he said. "Go away, you hairy, horrible wolf."

"Very well then," the wolf replied. "I'll huff and I'll puff and I'll blow your house down."

The wolf blew and he blew and he blew. Clouds of straw were sent flying up into the air and the house fell down.

The poor little pig had no protection from the wolf and ran as fast as he could to the second pig's wooden house. They closed all the windows, and pushed a chair up against the door. Then they huddled together, shaking with fear.

The wolf didn't take long to find them.

"Little pigs, little pigs, let me come in," said the wolf.

"No way," said the second little pig. "Go away, you hairy, old wolf."

"Oh no I won't," the wolf replied. "I'll huff and I'll puff and I'll blow your house down."

The wolf blew and he blew and he blew. Sure enough the planks of wood began to loosen and crack, and the house fell down.

There was no time to hang about. Both pigs ran as fast as they could to the third pig's brick house. The third pig told them both not to worry. But the wolf was outside. He was desperately hungry now and the little pigs could hear his stomach grumbling. Only the third

pig was not scared, so the other two held on to him for comfort.

"Little pigs, little pigs, let me come in," said the wolf.

"You don't scare me," shouted the third pig. "Go away, you hairy, old wolf."

The wolf was angry now, but he knew that this was the last house. If he could get inside this house he would not be hungry for long.

"I'll huff and I'll puff and I'll blow your house down," he said.

So the wolf blew and he blew and he blew. But the bricks would not budge. So he blew and he blew and he blew again, until his cheeks ached and his sides split. But the bricks would not budge. The hairy, old wolf choked, and then gasped, and then sighed. Finally he collapsed in a heap on the ground. The brick house had beaten him.

The pigs held hands and danced about and had a party to celebrate. No more wolves came visiting, and from that day forward the little pigs all lived together in the brick house. They were much happier that way.

Jack and the Beanstalk

Once upon a time, there was a widow who lived with her son, Jack. They were so poor that they had to sell everything they owned. Soon all they had left was their cow, Daisy.

"I will take Daisy to market and get a good price for her," said Jack.

On the way to town, Jack met an old man who exclaimed, "What a fine cow. Here are some magic beans in exchange for her."

"What a great deal!" thought Jack, taking the beans.

He ran home to show his mother, but she was furious.

"Jack, what have you done?" she asked. "What use are a few beans? They won't fill our tummies."
She snatched the beans and threw them out of the window. Then she sent Jack to bed without any supper.

Next morning, when he opened his curtains, Jack saw something amazing. The magic beans had grown into a huge beanstalk. It was so tall he couldn't see the top. Jack ran into the garden and began climbing the beanstalk. Up and up he went, through the clouds.

As he climbed, Jack found himself in a magical world. Far in the distance he could see a huge castle. He stepped off the beanstalk and walked up to the castle. Opening a huge, wooden door, Jack slipped inside.

He tiptoed into a hall where there were chairs as big as mountains. Jack came to a kitchen, where he found a loaf of bread as big as a car. Hungrily, Jack broke off a handful of the bread to eat. *Cluck, cluck.* Looking about him, Jack saw a brown hen in a cage high up on a table.

"Take care," whispered the hen. "This is a giant's castle. If he finds you, he will gobble you up for sure."

"Who are you?" Jack asked, puzzled to find a talking hen.

"I am a magic hen. I lay golden eggs," the hen replied. "If you help me to escape from this castle I will gladly lay golden eggs for you."

Excited, Jack climbed up the leg of the table and crawled along the table top towards the hen's cage. But just as he was opening the cage, the walls of the castle began to shake.

"Is that an earthquake?" asked Jack.

"That's the giant," cried the hen. "Hide!"

Jack leapt behind a pepper pot that stood on the table. Into the kitchen strode a massive giant who roared,

"FEE, FI, FO, FUM,
I SMELL THE BLOOD
OF AN ENGLISHMAN.
BE HE ALIVE, OR BE HE DEAD,
I'LL GRIND HIS BONES
TO MAKE MY BREAD!"

The giant searched everywhere for the intruder. When he couldn't find Jack, the giant became so angry that he banged his fist down on the table. The pepper pot flew up into the air spilling pepper everywhere. Jack flew up into the air with it. He landed back on the table, right in front of the giant. Jack had to think quickly. He kicked the heap of pepper on the table into the giant's face. Wrinkling up his nose, the giant sneezed a hurricane-force sneeze that blew Jack and the hen out of the kitchen.

Struggling to his feet, Jack picked up the hen and sprinted toward the beanstalk. As he clambered down the beanstalk, the giant followed. When at last Jack reached the ground, he ran to the cottage and grabbed an axe. He chopped and chopped at the beanstalk. With a loud crack, it toppled over, and the giant tumbled to the ground, dead.

The magic hen was so glad to be free that it laid hundreds of golden eggs. Jack and his mother grew very rich and lived happily every after.

The Hare and the Tortoise

Once upon a time, there was a tortoise who lived a quiet, happy life. He didn't really care what he had to do, as long as he could do it at his own pace. That meant he did everything very, very slowly.

One day the tortoise was out for a very slow stroll, when suddenly something went *Zooooom!* There was a cloud of dust and then nothing. Nobody was there.

"Perhaps I imagined it," thought the tortoise lazily. He walked on, but for a second time something went *Zooooom!* A cloud of dust appeared again, and then nothing.

"What is it?" he wondered. "It's moving ever so fast." He walked on again. *Zooooom!* This time the dust settled and in front of the tortoise stood a tall brown hare.

"Howdy doody, slowcoach," said the hare. "What you doin'? Where you goin'? Huh? Huh?"

"Doing?" asked the tortoise. "Going? I was just taking a quiet stroll."

"A stroll? That's so boring," laughed the hare. "You should run and rush and *Zooooom!* Look. I'll show you."

The hare zoomed here and zoomed there and soon everything was covered in a big cloud of dust.

"You see! You see!" said the hare. "That's the way to do it.

26

Run! Rush! Zoom!"

"Hmmm," said the tortoise. "I'm happy going at my own pace, thank you very much."

"How can you live without speed, man?" asked the hare.

"I get by," said the tortoise.

"Loser!" laughed the hare.

"Oh, I wouldn't say that," argued the tortoise.

"I bet you've never won anything in your life," said the hare. "I've seen snails move faster than you."

"How about a race then?" asked the tortoise quietly.

"Ha ha!" laughed the hare. "Ha ha! A race? You and me?"

"That's what I said," replied the tortoise. "A race."

"You're on," said the hare, still laughing to himself. "This is going to be the easiest race I've ever run."

They decided they would race to the old oak tree on the top of the hill.

"Ready," said the hare.

"Steady," said the tortoise.

"Go!" shouted the hare and – *Zooooom!* – he was gone.

The hare was so fast that he almost overtook himself.

"This is so easy," he thought. "I could run backward and still win."

28

So he turned around and ran backward for a little while. But then he got bored.

"This is so easy. I could hop on one leg and still win." So he hopped along on one leg for a little while, but then he got bored of that too.

"This is so easy. I could have a sleep for a while and still win." So the hare lay down and closed his eyes. Soon he was fast asleep.

Meanwhile the tortoise was plodding along at his usual pace. As he walked, he looked at the blue sky and the birds in the trees, but he never stopped once. He was a little surprised when he found the hare asleep, but he didn't wake him as he passed by. Soon the tortoise was at the hill with the oak tree.

The hare woke up and yawned.

"What a great sleep," he thought. "Boy, I'm a great sleeper. I bet I sleep better than anyone else." Then he remembered the race. "Oh no!" he cried. *Zooooom*! He ran as fast as he could towards the old oak tree on the top of the hill, but he was too late. The tortoise was already there. The tortoise had won the race.

"Hello, Hare," said the tortoise. "What took you so long?"

"I don't believe it!" gasped the hare. "You can't have won! I'm the fastest. You are a slowcoach!"

The tortoise smiled and sang a little song:
"You might have a lot of pace,
But slow and steady wins the race."

The Fox and the Grapes

Once upon a time, there was a young fox who lived with her family in a big forest. She was a selfish little fox. Her mother and her father spent all day looking for tasty snacks for her. She was used to getting everything she wanted.

But not today. Today, it was summer and the forest was hot, even in the shadiest places. The fox's parents were away looking for food. The fox was all on her own and thirsty. She licked her dry lips. She wanted a drink, but the nearest stream was a long walk away and she was far too lazy to travel such a distance.

Looking around her, the fox saw a clearing in the forest. High in the trees she saw grape vines twisting and climbing through the branches, their leaves trailing to the floor. Unfortunately, all of the grapes that were easy to reach had been eaten by the other animals who lived in the forest. All that was left was one big bunch of grapes hanging high up from a vine that was looped over the top branch of the tallest tree.

"Those grapes look good to me," thought the fox. "Delicious, red, plump and juicy."
She had tasted grapes before and knew how wonderfully refreshing they would be to eat.

She could imagine the sweet juice on her tongue and the grape skins crunching between her teeth. "I won't be thirsty for much longer," the little fox thought.

The easiest thing was simply to jump up and grab them, so she leapt as high as she could. She snapped at the grapes with her teeth, but they were just out of reach and she missed them.

"Oh no," she moaned. Next, she went to the foot of the tall tree where the bunch of grapes grew. She tried to climb up its smooth trunk, but she wasn't a very good climber. Her paws were much more suited to the forest floor. She kept slipping, and soon she fell to the ground with a bump.

She sat for a moment on the forest floor looking up at the bunch of grapes. How delicious they looked, but so far away.

"Red and plump and juicy," she kept saying to herself. Her stomach grumbled. She wanted them more than anything and she was a fox who was used to getting her own way.

Eventually she decided to try to jump again, and this time she made an extra big effort. She trotted to the edge of the clearing. Then she turned and ran as fast as she could toward the tree. When she reached top speed, she pushed with her paws and took off.

Up, up she went, higher than she had ever jumped before. The grapes hung on the vine and as she felt herself getting closer and closer. She was sure she could smell them. She snapped with her teeth, but felt only thin air.

With a crash she tumbled to the ground and rolled over. She lay for a while, feeling very sorry for herself. She was bruised and tired, angry and fed up. She had had enough. She looked at the grapes one last time and then turned away and stalked out of the clearing with her nose in the air.

"I don't care," she sneered. "They were probably sour, anyway." And that is how the fox lived for the rest of her life, always pretending she didn't like the things she couldn't have.

Goldilocks and the Three Bears

Once upon a time, there was a little girl called Goldilocks. She had nobody to play with, so she spent her days on her own, combing her long golden hair. One day she put her comb down and went for a walk in the woods. More than anything she wanted to find someone to be her friend. Before long she came across a little cottage that belonged to a family of bears.

"I wonder if anyone is at home?" she thought. She looked through the window, but there was nobody inside. She knocked on the door and it opened a little. Feeling naughty but quite brave, she crept inside.

In the kitchen she found three bowls of soup. The first was a big bowl and belonged to Father Bear. The second was a middle-sized bowl and belonged to Mother Bear. The third bowl was tiny. It belonged to Baby Bear.

Goldilocks was feeling hungry and couldn't resist trying some of the soup. First, she ate some soup from the big bowl.

"Yuck," she said, throwing down the spoon. "Too much pepper."

Next she tried some soup from the middle-sized bowl.

"Yuck," she said. "Too much salt."

Lastly, she tried the soup from the tiny bowl.

"Yum. That tastes just right," she said, and ate it all up.

Next, Goldilocks found three chairs. The first was a big chair and belonged to Father Bear. The second was a middle-sized chair and belonged to Mother Bear. The third chair was Baby Bear's. It was tiny.

First, Goldilocks sat in the big chair.

"Oh no," she said. "That's much too hard."

Next, she tried the middle chair.

"Oh no," she said. "That's much too soft."

Lastly, she tried the tiny chair.

"Ooh yes," she said. "That's just right."

But just as she relaxed in the tiny chair, one of its legs broke off. Oh dear, what a mess she was making!

Goldilocks went upstairs to the bedroom where she found three beds – Father Bear's big bed, Mother Bear's middle-sized bed and Baby Bear's tiny bed.

Can you guess which was the most comfortable? Goldilocks lay down on Baby Bear's tiny bed and fell fast asleep.

It wasn't long before the family of bears arrived home. When they went into the kitchen they got a mighty surprise.

"Who's been tasting my soup?" asked Father Bear.

35

"Who's been tasting my soup?" asked Mother Bear.

"Tasting? Someone has eaten up all my soup!" Baby
Bear cried.

Next they saw their chairs.

"Who's been sitting in my chair?" asked Father Bear.

"Who's been sitting in my chair?" asked Mother Bear.

"Sitting? Someone has broken a leg off my chair!"
Baby Bear cried again.

The three bears stomped upstairs. They were shocked
to find a lovely little girl in Baby Bear's bed. Goldilocks
was fast asleep, but she soon woke up to find three
angry bears growling at her.

"I'm sorry," said Goldilocks, jumping out of bed.
"I promise I won't come into your house again."
Father Bear and Mother Bear were very angry.

"What are we going to do with her?" they said.

Baby Bear looked at Goldilocks. He had never seen
such beautiful golden hair. Moreover, he had never had
a friend come to play at his house before.

"I think we should forgive her," he suggested.

Goldilocks was very relieved. From that day on, she
came back to the house whenever she could. She and
Baby Bear played together and became best friends,
but she was always very careful with his toys.

The Elves and the Shoemaker

There once lived a kind shoemaker who worked very hard but was terribly poor. One day, all he had left was a piece of leather big enough to make one pair of shoes. He cut the shape of a pair of shoes from the leather and left it on his work-table ready to sew in the morning.

The next day he woke up and went downstairs to start work. For a moment, the shoemaker wondered if he was dreaming. On the work-table was a pair of shoes. They were beautiful. Every stitch was perfect.

"Who has made these marvellous shoes?" he wondered. At that moment a customer came to visit the shoemaker. She saw the shoes and bought them straightaway, paying the shoemaker enough money to buy food and two pieces of leather for two more pairs of shoes.

That night, the shoemaker laid the leather out on his work-table. The next morning, instead of the piece of leather, he found two pairs of shoes, even more beautiful than the day before. His first customers of the day bought them immediately.

The shoemaker now had enough money to buy four pieces of leather for four pairs of shoes. He laid the leather out on his table and by morning it had been transformed into more wonderful shoes.

Day after day the miracle continued. News of the fine shoes spread quickly and soon the shoemaker was the richest man in town.

One evening the shoemaker and his wife were discussing their good fortune.

"I still can't work it out," said his wife. "What kind of magic has been making the shoes?"

"I have no idea," replied the shoemaker. "But I want to find out."

So that night the shoemaker laid out the leather on his work-table. Then he and his wife hid behind a curtain and waited. When the clock struck midnight, two small elves, barefoot and dressed in ragged clothes, tiptoed into the workshop. They sat down on the work-table and began making the leather into shoes. Their tiny hands and fingers worked quickly, making perfect, tiny stitches.

They must have been cold in their rags, but they worked hard until all the shoes were finished. Then they slipped out of the workshop and disappeared into the night.

The shoemaker and his wife were extremely grateful to the elves.

"Those little elves have made us rich," said the shoemaker's wife. "We must do something for them in return. I'm going to make them some new clothes,"

"And I shall make them both a new pair of shoes," said the shoemaker.

They worked all day, making two tiny green outfits and two pairs of tiny leather shoes. When the clothes and shoes were finished, the shoemaker and his wife put them on the work-table, and hid behind the curtain.

At midnight, the door opened, and in came the two elves. When they saw the tiny clothes and shoes they laughed with delight. They took off their ragged old clothes and put on the new ones. They pulled on their new shoes and danced with delight.

"This is the best present ever!" they squealed. They were so happy that they danced out of the workshop and skipped down the street.

The shoemaker and his wife never saw the elves again, but they were so rich now that they never had to work another day. Sometimes, when the clock struck twelve, the shoemaker would lie awake and remember the elves dancing in their new shoes. It was the proudest moment of his life.

The Billy Goats Gruff

Once upon a time, there were three billy-goat brothers named Gruff. There was Big Billy Goat Gruff, who was the oldest and, of course, the biggest. There was Middle-sized Billy Goat Gruff, and Little Billy Goat Gruff, who was the youngest and the smallest. They lived in a rocky valley. When spring came, they began to search for grass to eat. They jumped from one rock to another, but couldn't find enough to fill their stomachs.

High on the mountainside above the valley, the brothers could see a beautiful green pasture, with tall, lush grass. It made their empty stomachs rumble.

"Let's climb the mountain to find some sweet grass to eat," suggested Big Billy Goat Gruff.

Off they set. By lunchtime, they had reached a rushing river that was impossible to cross without using the rickety bridge that stretched across it. But under the bridge lived a troll – a rotten-toothed, wart-nosed, billy goat-eating troll, which is the worst kind.

Little Billy Goat Gruff was the first to cross the bridge. *Trip trap, trip trap, trippety-trippety trap*, went his hooves as he skipped across. *Tinkle, tinkle* went the tiny bell around his neck.

"Who is that skipping over my bridge?" growled the troll from under the planks.

"It is only me," said Little Billy Goat Gruff.

"I am going to gobble you up," threatened the troll.

"Please Mr. Troll, don't eat me. I am tiny and bony. I won't taste very good. Wait for my brother. He is bigger and much tastier."

"All right," snarled the troll. "You can cross my bridge today, but I'll eat you when you return from the pasture, round and fat." So Little Billy Goat Gruff made it to the other side of the river.

Next came Middle-sized Billy Goat Gruff. *Trip trap, trip trap, trippety-trippety trap*, went his hooves as he trotted across. *Ding, dong* went the bell around his neck.

"Who is that trotting over my bridge?" shouted the troll, shaking the bridge with his slimy, green arms.

"It is only me," said Middle-sized Billy Goat Gruff.

"I am going to gobble you up," threatened the troll.

"Please Mr. Troll, don't eat me. I am only a middle-sized billy goat and not big enough for your lunch. Wait for my brother. He is bigger than me and much tastier."

"Today is your lucky day. I'll let you cross my bridge, but I'll eat you when you return from the pasture, round and fat," said the troll. So Middle-sized Billy Goat Gruff reached the other side of the river.

Last came Big Billy Goat Gruff. *TRIP TRAP, TRIP TRAP, BISH BASH BOSH* went his great big hooves as he stomped across. *CLANG, CLANG* went the huge bell slung around his neck.

"Who is that stomping over my bridge?" roared the troll, glaring through the planks of the bridge with his one eye which was the size of a big, juicy watermelon.

"I'm their BIG BROTHER," came the reply.

"At last!" roared the troll. "I'm going to gobble you up." And he leapt onto the bridge.

"OK. I think you'll find I'm big enough to eat," laughed Big Billy Goat Gruff, and he lowered his head, aiming his two great horns at the troll. He galloped along the bridge, lifted the troll with his long horns and tossed him up into the air. Down tumbled the troll into the swirling river and he was never seen again.

"Let's go," said Big Billy Goat Gruff. So the brothers trotted up to the pasture, where they ate lush, green grass all summer long, until they were round and fat and full.

The Emperor's New Clothes

In a beautiful land, far away, lived a mighty emperor – a mighty emperor who absolutely loved clothes. He loved to wear fabulous suits that were the height of fashion, and would spend all of his money on them. He had a new outfit for every hour of every day.

One day, two strangers appeared at the gates of the palace. They asked the guards to deliver a message.

"Tell the emperor that we are the finest tailors in the world. We will make him the greatest suit in the history of great suits. It will be made from an amazing new cloth – a cloth so fine that only very wise men can see it. To idiots and fools it will seem invisible."

The guard rushed through the corridors of the palace. He found the emperor in the royal bedroom, trying on a pair of shoes decorated with rubies as big as cherries.

"I must have this suit as soon as possible," the emperor cried, rubbing his hands together with glee. "Bring the tailors to me."

When the tailors were brought before him, they bowed elegantly.

"Here are two hundred pieces of gold," said the emperor. "Buy all the thread you need to make my suit." Secretly he thought, "What a wonderful piece of luck.

45

Not only will I be the best-dressed man around, but I can use this suit to prove just how brilliantly clever I am. I'll find out which of my courtiers are clever enough to serve me."

The tailors were shown out of the royal bedroom. The moment the doors were closed, they burst out laughing. Tears rolled down their faces and they had to lean against the wall to stop themselves from falling over. They weren't really tailors at all. They were villains who had come to trick the emperor.
They hid the gold coins and set up their looms. Whenever anybody passed by they pretended to be busy weaving cloth with their wonderful thread, but in fact there was no thread there at all.

As the days passed, the emperor grew more and more desperate to see what the cloth looked like. He decided to send his prime minister to check on the tailors' progress. The prime minister strolled into the workroom, and was struck dumb. He saw the two tailors busy at their looms, but no matter how hard he looked, he couldn't see the cloth. "Oh no!" he thought. "Can this mean I'm a fool?"

  "Prime Minister," said one of the tailors. "What do you think of the pattern we have chosen? Will the emperor like it?"
Terrified that they might guess he couldn't see what they were pointing at, the prime minister replied, "Oh, it's fabulous. I will definitely tell his Highness that it is the finest cloth I have ever seen."

The second tailor began to describe the imaginary cloth, boasting about the genius of every detail and stitch. The prime minister listened carefully, making sure that he would be able to repeat every word to the emperor.

"Tell the emperor that we need one hundred more pieces of gold to buy more thread," added the first tailor, trying not to smile.

When the emperor heard about the beauty of the cloth, he insisted on seeing it himself. Followed by ten courtiers, who scurried to keep up with him, he marched through the palace to visit the tailors. But when he entered their workroom he was horrified. He couldn't see anything.

Surely the looms were empty, or was he – the greatest emperor in the history of some pretty great emperors – an idiot?

"It's perfect!" he declared.

The courtiers stared at him open-mouthed. But then one muttered, "Incredible!" Another said, "Delightful!" "Magnificent!" a third shouted.

As you can imagine, once the royal party had left, the tailors laughed and laughed until their sides hurt. This was just too easy.

48

Soon everyone in the city was talking about the amazing cloth. They couldn't wait to see the emperor's new suit. Secretly, however, all of them were terrified that they wouldn't be able to see it.

At last the day of the great procession arrived. The emperor visited the tailors for the final fitting of his new suit. Feeling a little shy, he undressed right down to his polka dot underwear and admired himself in the mirror.

"Oh Sir, to make sure the suit fits perfectly you must take everything off," insisted the tailors.

Gulping and looking around nervously at all the courtiers, the emperor pulled off the rest of his clothes. The tailors fussed around him, pretending to help him into the imaginary suit.

"A perfect fit," they cried.

"Yes," agreed the prime minister. "A triumph, Majesty – your finest suit yet."

The emperor began to smile.

"Time to show my people," he declared.

It was a fantastic procession, with dancers, jugglers and musicians. The emperor rode his finest horse and the prime minister led the way. The crowd cheered and waved flags and banners. But as soon as they saw the emperor, the crowd fell silent. You could have heard a tailor's needle drop. Anxiously, people looked at each other, checking whether they were the only ones who were so foolish that they couldn't see the emperor's new clothes.

"What beautiful cloth!" a young man shouted.

"What amazing patterns!" a road sweeper cheered.

"What beautiful buttons!" shouted an old lady who was selling eggs.

"But Dad…" said a little boy, watching the procession. "…Dad! The emperor's not wearing any clothes. He's not wearing anything at all. He's… naked!"

A gasp went through the crowd. But then there was a murmur, then a whisper, a snort and a giggle. One man began to chuckle. Another roared with laughter.

It was true – the emperor really was naked.

Horrified, the poor emperor grabbed the prime minister's cloak. Turning his horse around, he galloped all the way back to the palace and hid in his bedroom. He had been tricked. He, Emperor Maximus Magnifico, was the biggest fool in the land.

Of course, by the time the emperor sent the army to arrest the two tailors, they were nowhere to be seen. They had taken all the gold and escaped over the border, out of his reach forever.

The Wolf and the Seven Little Kids

Once upon a time, in a little cottage beside a huge forest, lived Mother Goat and her seven little kids. All summer long the kids frolicked in the fields without a care in the world. But deep in the forest lurked a wily, whisker-faced wolf. Every day he spied on the tasty-looking kids.

"Yum, yum," he muttered under his bad breath. "Kid-burgers for my lunch."

One day, Mother Goat decided to visit her sister on the other side of the forest. She gathered the kids around her. "While I'm away you must promise not to let the wolf into the cottage," she said.

All seven kids shivered when she mentioned the wolf.

"How long will you be gone?" the youngest asked.

"Not for long, my darling," she replied. "But when I return, I will place my milky-white hooves on the windowsill. Then you will know it is me." With that she trotted off into the forest.

At first the kids tiptoed nervously around the house, flinching at every creak and groan. But soon they forgot the dangers that lurked outside, and began chasing each other around the kitchen, playing hide and seek. Silently, the wolf crept toward the cottage. Not even a blade of grass whispered to warn the kids he was coming.

KNOCK, KNOCK, KNOCK!

"Who's there?" whimpered the kids.

"It's your mother. I am back from my trip," growled the wolf in his gruff voice.

All seven kids rolled on the floor with laughter.

"Forget it, Mr. Wolf. You don't sound like our mother." Pounding his forehead with frustration, the wolf stalked back into the forest, his stomach rumbling with hunger.

Half an hour later the kids heard another *KNOCK, KNOCK, KNOCK!*

"Who's there?" they shouted, a little braver than before.

"Your loving mother," sang the wolf in a voice as sweet as honey. "I've walked through the forest and I'm tired. I want to come in and rest."

"That's not the wolf, it's Mother," shouted the youngest kid. "We must let her in."

"Not before we have seen her hooves," said the eldest kid, who was feeling very calm and sensible.

"Mother, put your hooves up on the windowsill, so we can be sure it's you." Moments later a huge pair of paws with big, sharp claws appeared on the windowsill.

"Yuck! Those aren't Mother's hooves. They are horny and hairy and smelly," squealed the kids. "Our mother has beautiful, dainty hooves, that are as white as snow. Mr. Wolf, you're not coming in here. Never, ever, *ever!*" They danced around the kitchen, leaping over each other, delighted at how clever they were. With his feelings hurt and his stomach empty, the wolf slunk back into the forest.

An hour later the kids heard a gentle tap at the door.

"Who's there?" they called.

"Your mother," said a gentle voice. "I've returned from a long and thirsty journey. Please let me in. Here are my beautiful, milky white hooves. See how white they are." And sure enough a pair of milky white paws appeared on the windowsill. What the kids couldn't know was that the wolf had dipped his paws into a barrel of flour to make them white.

"That's our mother," said the eldest kid.

"Are you sure?" asked the youngest kid. "Those hooves are awfully big."

"Of course I'm sure, and anyway, I'm the eldest," her big brother replied.

So the kids slid back the bolt and flung the door open. In the blink of an eye the wolf leapt into the kitchen. He pounced on the eldest kid and swallowed him whole. He gobbled up the second kid… "Delicious!"… the third… "Yummy!"… the fourth… "Best yet!" the fifth… "Mmmm," and the sixth… "*Burp!* Excuse me!" Then he looked around him a little confused. "I'm sure there were seven kids. Never mind, I'm stuffed," he declared, and lumbered out of the cottage. When he reached a clearing in the woods, the wolf stretched out and fell fast asleep. He snored so loudly that all the forest animals had to cover their ears.

Later that day Mother Goat returned from her trip. When she reached the cottage, she found the door of the cottage wide open and could see no sign of her seven children.

"What has happened to my babies?" she cried. Hearing her mother's sobs, the youngest kid, who was hiding inside the clock case, shouted, "Here I am!" She scooped the kid up in her arms and hugged her.

"Where are your brothers and sisters?" she asked.

"Mother, the wolf tricked us all. We thought you had come home and we opened the door. Now all my brothers and sisters are inside the wolf," squealed the youngest kid. "He swallowed them whole."

Mother Goat ran into the forest. Before long she heard the wolf's snores echoing through the trees – *ZZZzzzZZZ*. Then she spied him lying on his back, sound asleep, his hairy belly bulging with his lunch.

57

She took her scissors, a needle and some thread from her basket and snipped the wolf open. Out popped the six kids. Overjoyed to see their mother again, they crowded around her all talking at once.

"Hush," she whispered. Placing six huge stones inside the wolf, Mother Goat quickly sewed him up again. Then they all tiptoed to the edge of the clearing and hid. Eight pairs of eyes watched the wolf snoozing.

At last the wolf yawned and burped.

"Mmm, after a tasty feast and a little doze, I'd like a long, cool drink," he decided. So he staggered toward the river. His big belly, which was full of stones, swayed from side to side as he walked. Quietly, Mother Goat and her seven kids followed him.

At the edge of the river the wolf bent down to drink.

"*CHARGE!*" shouted Mother Goat and all the kids galloped toward the wolf. They butted and they barged until he tumbled into the swirling water. Down he sank, the stones in his tummy dragging him deeper, until he was gone.

Mother Goat and her seven little kids skipped all the way home and had cake to celebrate.

Rumpelstiltskin

Once upon a time, there lived a miller who had a beautiful daughter called Leonora. One day, as he was delivering flour to the castle, he met the king. The miller, who was a terrible show-off, bowed to the king.

"Good morning, Majesty," he said. "I don't like to boast, but my daughter is so talented that she can spin straw into gold."

"Fascinating," said the king. "Bring your daughter to the castle tomorrow morning so I can see her talents for myself."

The miller was horrified because his boast was not true. But there was nothing he could do. So he took Leonora to the castle. The king led her to a chamber full of straw. In one corner of the room was a spinning wheel.

"Get to work," ordered the king. "If you haven't spun all this straw to gold by morning, I'll have your head cut off." With that he closed the door.

Leonora sat down and began to weep. She had no idea how to spin straw into gold. But suddenly the door flew open and a strange little man appeared. He had crooked legs, a long red nose and a beard that was so long it was tied in a knot.

"Good evening," he chirped. "Why are you crying?"

"The king wants me to spin all this straw into gold, but I don't know how," cried Leonora.

"What will you give me if I do it for you?" asked the little man.

"My necklace," offered Leonora.

Pleased with this bargain, the little man sat down and started to spin. *Whirr, whirr,* went the spinning wheel, and the little man's fingers moved so quickly that all Leonora could see was a blur. By morning, every piece of the straw in the room had been turned into gold.

When the king returned in the morning he was delighted. He was a greedy man, however, and wanted more gold. He took Leonora to a bigger room full of straw.

"Here is a spinning wheel, here is some straw. If you haven't spun all of it into gold by morning, I will have your head cut off," he threatened.

As soon as she was alone, Leonora began to cry again. But the door sprang open and in came the little man.

"What will you give me this time if I spin the straw into gold?" he asked.

"My ring," suggested Leonora.

With a satisfied smile he sat down and began to spin. By sunrise all the straw had been turned to pure gold.

When the king arrived, he clapped his hands with delight. But still he wanted more gold. He led Leonora into an even bigger room. It was so full of straw that the piles almost touched the ceiling.

61

"If you haven't spun all the straw into gold by morning... well, you know what will happen. If you succeed, I will make you my queen," promised the king.

As soon as the king left the room, the little man appeared, laughing and dancing around Leonora.

"What will you give me this time? What will you give me?" he asked.

"I've got nothing left to give," wailed Leonora.

"Then you must promise me that when you are queen you will give me your first baby," said the little man. Leonora could see no other way to save her life, so she gave him her word. He set to work and spun all the straw into gold. When the king saw the enormous heap of gold, he married Leonora straightaway.

A year passed before Leonora had a beautiful baby. She forgot all about her promise to the little man until one day he crept into her room.

"I have come for my prize," he demanded. Leonora was terrified. She offered him all the riches in the kingdom instead. But the little man shook his head.

"You must keep your promise," he said. Leonora wept so bitterly that the little man began to feel sorry for her.

"I will give you three days to guess my name," he said. "If you guess it correctly, you can keep your baby. If not, the baby will be mine."

Leonora sent a messenger throughout the kingdom to write down all the names he came across. She lay awake at night, thinking of all the names she had ever heard.

When the little man arrived the next day, Leonora recited all the names she knew.

"Are you called Albert?"

"No, that's not my name."

"Are you called Andrew?"

"No."

"Arthur?"

"Nope."

Even when she got to Zebedee, the little man still said,

"No, that is not my name."

The next day, Leonora asked everybody in the castle to suggest more names. When the little man appeared she had a list of some really extraordinary names.

"Is your name Sheepshanks, Hedwig or Shockles?" she asked, but he always replied, "No."

On the third day the messenger who had been sent to collect names returned to the castle.

"I have not been able to find any new names," he admitted. "But as I was riding through a forest, I saw a cottage. In front of it was a bonfire, and around the fire the strangest little man was dancing. He had crooked legs, a long red nose and a beard that was so long he had tied it in a knot. As he hopped and jumped, he sang this song.

'My dancing and singing I will do today,
For tomorrow the queen's son I will take away.
All the queen's riches and all the queen's fame,
Will not help her guess Rumpelstiltskin's my name.'

Leonora clapped her hands with joy.

When the little man came to the castle and asked her
what his name was, she asked, "Is your name Rufus?"

"No," he answered.

"Is your name Conrad?"

"No."

"Is your name Rumpelstiltskin?"

"Who told you that?" screamed the little man. "Was
it the elves? Was it the trolls?" In a rage, he stamped his
foot so hard it went straight into the ground. This made
him even angrier. He grabbed his foot to pull it out of
the ground, but pulled so hard he tore himself in two.
And that was the end of Rumpelstiltskin.

The Tiger, the Old Man and the Jackal

Long ago, in a tiny village in India, a wicked tiger terrorized the villagers. He gave their children nightmares and ate their cattle. One day, seven brave villagers decided to stop the tiger. They made a huge net and hid behind some bushes. When the tiger stalked into the village, they threw their net at him. The tiger became so tangled and tied in the net that he couldn't escape. Then the villagers locked him in a great wooden cage. The tiger snarled and spat, but he could not get out.

One day, an old man was passing the cage. Hearing a terrible moan, he peered through the bars.

"Old man," the tiger called. "Take pity on me. My throat is so dry. Please let me out of this cage for a moment, so I can drink some cool water from the river."

"I'm no fool," snorted the old man. "The moment I let you out, you will eat me whole."

"No, how could you say that? All I want is a drink," promised the tiger. "I would not be that ungrateful to the man who saves my life."

"Do you promise?" asked the old man.

"Yes," nodded the tiger.

Sliding back the heavy bolt, the old man opened the

66

door of the cage. The tiger sprang out.

"Now I am going to eat you up," he roared.

"But you promised!" shrieked the terrified old man. "Tiger, I beg you, spare my life. Would you really eat the man who set you free?"

"Actually, I would," admitted the tiger.

"Give me a moment to think," begged the old man. "I know. Let's ask five creatures whether they think it is fair that you eat me. If they do, I am willing to die."

"Very well," agreed the tiger, licking his lips.

Off they set, looking for someone to ask. First, they came to a tall banyan tree growing beside the road.

"Banyan Tree," called the old man. "Do you think it is fair that Tiger eats me, even though I let him out of the cage?"

"Well," said the banyan tree, in his gloomy voice. "At noon, when the sun is high, humans rest in the shade of my leafy branches. But when evening comes, and they are no longer hot and bothered, they break off my twigs to make fires. They show me no gratitude. So I say yes, let Tiger eat you."

Tiger smiled and licked his lips.

"Let's walk a little further," said the old man quickly. On they went until they met a camel.

"Camel," said the old man. "Do you think it is fair that Tiger gobbles me up even though I let him out of the cage?"

"All my life I have worked hard for my master," grumbled the camel. "Now that I am old and slow, he makes me work harder than ever, and beats me every day. My master is not fair to me. So I say yes, let Tiger eat you."

"Eagle!" shouted the old man nervously. "Do you think it is fair that Tiger gobbles me up?"
The eagle swooped down and landed at their feet.

"I am a bird of the sky and I have never harmed a human. Yet they steal the eggs from my nest and shoot me with their arrows. Humans are cruel. So I say yes, let Tiger eat you."

The tiger prepared to pounce.

"Wait!" squealed the old man. "We agreed to ask two more creatures."

On the riverbank they found a grinning alligator, sunning himself.

"Please, Alligator, do you think it is fair that Tiger gobbles me up, even though I let him out of the cage?"

69

Hissing through his razor-sharp teeth, the alligator whispered, "Every day I have to hide in the mud from humans who want to catch me and kill me. So I say yes, let Tiger eat you."

The old man had only one more chance. Soon they met a jackal, scampering along the road.

"Jackal, you are my last chance." said the old man. "Do you think it is fair that Tiger gobbles me up even though I was kind enough to let him out of the cage?"

"What are you talking about?" asked the jackal, puzzled.

"I found Tiger locked up in a cage," the old man explained. "He begged me to let him out so he could drink some water. But as soon as he was out, he threatened to eat me. Do you think that is fair?"

"What kind of cage was it?" asked the jackal.

"A large wooden one," replied the old man.

"And you let him out?"

"Yes, I did."

"I'm afraid I can't really imagine this. Would you take me to the cage, so that I can see it myself?" asked the jackal.

So together they walked back to the cage.

"Old man," said the jackal. "Exactly where were you standing when Tiger asked you to help him?"

"About here," said the old man.

"And you, Tiger, where were you exactly?" asked the jackal.

"Stuck inside the cage," complained the tiger.

"Bear with me a little longer," begged the jackal.

"I still can't quite picture the situation. Were you skulking at the back of the cage or prowling near the bars? Would you pop back into the cage and show me exactly where you were standing?"

"If I must," sighed the tiger, and slunk into the cage.

"And was the door open or shut when you were inside?" asked the jackal.

"Shut, of course," replied the tiger.

"Could we just demonstrate that for a moment?" asked the jackal.

"If we must," agreed the tiger.

The jackal swung the door shut.

"One last question. Was the door bolted?" he asked.

"Yes. Just like this," said the old man and he slid the heavy bolt across.

"Now that the door is bolted, old man, I think you should go home right away," said the jackal. "And you, Tiger, you are an ungrateful beast. The old man helped you, and in return you were going to eat him for your lunch. I hope you stay in that cage for a long, long time."

With that, the jackal and the old man turned and walked off toward the village. Inside the cage, the tiger moaned with frustration, because he had been tricked so easily.

The Twelve Dancing Princesses

Once upon a time, there was a shepherd boy called
Michael. One day, while watching his flock, he fell
asleep under an oak, and dreamed that a lady appeared
and said, "Go to the castle of Beloeil, and you shall
marry a princess." So he set off for Beloeil.

Twelve beautiful princesses lived in the castle. All twelve
girls slept in the same room and at night their door was
bolted, but every morning their shoes were found worn
and torn and full of holes.

73

When the king asked them what they had been doing all night, they always answered, "Only sleeping, father". At last, the king announced that the man who solved the mystery could choose one of the princesses for his wife. Many princes tried, but each one disappeared.

When Michael reached Beloeil, he asked the gardener for a job. His duty was to make bouquets that were given to the princesses every morning. When Lina, the youngest princess, saw Michael, she sighed.

"How pretty our new flower boy is!" she whispered. When Michael saw Lina, he fell in love straightaway.

That night, the lady came to him in a dream. In one hand she held a laurel tree and in the other a rake, a bucket and a silk towel.

"Plant this laurel," she said. "Rake it, water it, and wipe it with the towel. When it is as tall as you, say, 'Beautiful laurel, I have raked you and watered you.

I have wiped you with the silk towel.' Then ask for anything you choose, and it will be yours."

When Michael awoke, he found a laurel tree beside his bed. So he carefully obeyed the lady's instructions. The tree grew and grew. When it was as tall as him, Michael said, "Beautiful laurel, I have raked you and watered you. I have wiped you with the silk towel. I want to be invisible." Instantly, a white flower appeared on the laurel. Michael picked it and in the blink of an eye he became invisible.

That night, when the princesses went up to bed, Michael made himself invisible and followed them. He watched the girls open their wardrobes and each put on a magnificent dress and a new pair of satin shoes. The eldest clapped her hands and a secret door opened in the floor.

The sisters disappeared down a staircase. Michael followed. Down they went and through another door into a beautiful wood of trees with silver-spangled leaves. Next they came to a wood with gold-spangled leaves, and then a third where the leaves glittered with diamonds. The princesses walked until they reached a lake where twelve little boats were waiting. From a castle on the far shore came the sound of music and laughter. Each princess stepped into a boat and paddled across the lake. Unseen, Michael slipped into Lina's boat.

Inside the castle, the princesses went into a grand ballroom. Michael watched, envying every handsome young man who danced with Lina. The young men were all the princes who had tried to discover the princesses' secret.

The girls had given them a magic potion, which made them forget who they were, and live only to dance.

The princesses danced until their shoes were worn and torn and full of holes. Then they returned home. As they passed through the silver wood, Michael broke off a branch as proof of what he had seen. Then he slipped ahead of them. Running up the secret staircase, he flung open the bedroom window and slid down a vine to the ground.

That day, when he made the bouquets, Michael hid the silver branch in Lina's bouquet. She was very surprised, but said nothing.

That evening, Michael followed the sisters again. Lina looked for Michael, but she couldn't see him. As they came back from the ball, Michael broke off a branch with gold-spangled leaves.

Next day Lina found the branch in her bouquet. So she stayed behind.

"Where does this branch come from?" she whispered to Michael.

"I followed you," he replied.

"Please don't reveal our secret," begged Lina. But Michael said nothing.

The next night, as the princesses returned home from the ball, through the wood with diamond-spangled leaves, Lina heard a snapping sound and, sure enough, next morning the branch was in her bouquet.

"If you reveal our secret, you can choose one of us as your bride," Lina whispered to Michael,

"I know," answered Michael.

"Don't you want to marry one of us?" she asked. But Michael said nothing.

Lina's sisters saw her talking to the gardener's boy. They teased her until she told them that Michael knew where they went at night.

"He must be sent to the dungeon," said the eldest princess.

"No," Lina cried. "If you harm him, I will tell father our secret myself."

So they decided to take Michael to the ball and give him the magic potion that would enchant him. Michael, however, had made himself invisible and heard every word of their plan.

He went to the laurel tree and asked for clothes fit for a prince. A beautiful pink flower appeared. He picked it and found himself dressed in a fine, black, velvet tunic. So that night, Michael went with the princesses to the ball. He danced so gracefully that everyone was delighted with him. After supper, a page brought in a golden goblet.

"Michael," said the eldest sister. "You have discovered our secret. Let's drink to your triumph."

Michael took the goblet, looking at Lina as he raised it to his lips.

"Don't drink!" cried Lina. "I would rather marry a gardener than lose you."

Michael flung the goblet aside, and fell to his knees at Lina's feet. In a flash, the potion's power over all the princes in the ballroom was broken. Each princess chose one of the princes to be their husband, and together they returned to Beloeil.

Michael told the king what he had discovered. The king was delighted and was happy to grant him Princess Lina's hand in marriage, and Lina was delighted. But Lina did not become a gardener's wife, because the king made Michael a prince, and they lived happily ever after.

The Young Samurai

Once upon a time, in the country of Japan, there lived a prince. He came from a large, powerful family that had a long and noble history. He was both handsome and well liked. Women from all over the land wanted to marry the prince, but the one he liked best was a woman called Toya. He saw her as much as he could. They rode their horses in the country, and went for long walks together in the royal gardens.

When summer came, the prince and Toya went for picnics and read poetry to one another. One day they were sitting beneath a willow tree, when the prince asked Toya to marry him. Delighted, she said yes, and they were both so happy at their engagement that neither of them noticed a black cat following them.

The black cat was not a normal cat, not a household pet. This was a demon cat, a supernatural creature from the hills. It had a wicked walk and sinister smile, and it was only happy when everyone else was sad. Most of all, it hated seeing young people in love.

That night Toya went to her room. Looking around her, she was aware of something in the room. Suddenly, she saw, crouching at the end of her bed, the demon cat. Before Toya could cry out for help the cat sprang and grabbed her. It carried her out of the palace, through the shadows of the town and into the countryside. It took her up into the hills and left her in the corner of a deep, dark cave.

The cat was a "shape shifter", which means it could make itself look like any other creature it wanted. It could change itself into a horse, or a puppy and even into a person. When the cat returned to the palace, it changed itself to look exactly like Toya. The cat looked so like Toya that not even the prince could tell the difference, so he loved the false Toya by mistake.

They rode their horses together and went for walks in the royal gardens. He even read his poetry to her.

All the time the prince had no idea that he was with the demon cat. All the time he had no idea that the woman he had asked to marry him, the real Toya, was hidden in a cave in the hills.

However, the prince did notice that gradually he was growing weaker. He was tired all the time, and he found it difficult to get out of bed in the morning. His friends joked that it was because he was so much in love with Toya. But it was not long before the prince became very sick.

Doctors were brought to see him. They rubbed him with lotions and filled him with potions, but nothing worked. After a while, the doctors discovered that the prince suffered most during the night. He slept badly and had terrible nightmares.

The royal council met to discuss the problem. They decided that fifty servants should sit with the prince throughout the night while he was sleeping. Surely if there was anything wrong then fifty servants would find out?

The prince was so sick now that he didn't really notice the fifty servants who stood around his room. Unfortunately, the servants didn't notice the demon cat either. The creature appeared in the room and cast a magic spell so that just before midnight everyone became drowsy and fell fast asleep. When they were all asleep the demon cat disguised itself as Toya and cast a spell over the prince that gave him terrible nightmares until sunrise.

Night after night, the fifty servants came to watch over the prince. Always they fell asleep at midnight. Eventually even members of the royal council joined them, but they all fell asleep too. The demon cat's magic was very strong. The prince grew sicker and sicker and the royal council pulled their hair out, not knowing what to do.

At last, a holy man was asked to pray for the prince. He sat in his shrine room night after night praying for the prince to get well again. One night, while the holy man was praying particularly hard, he heard a strange noise from the garden. He looked out of the window

84

and saw a young samurai (because soldiers are known
as samurai in Japan) who was washing himself.

As he washed, the young samurai sang to himself. He
sang soldiers' songs and most of them were so funny that
they made the holy man laugh. When the young samurai
had finished his songs he stood before a shrine and
began to pray for the prince, asking the gods to help him
get well.

The holy man was very surprised to see how loyal the young samurai was. He called to the young samurai, who stood to attention.

"What is your name, young samurai?"

"I am Ito Soda," the samurai replied. "Infantry division, Sir."

"I heard you praying for the prince," said the holy man.

"That's true," said the young samurai. "I have heard of the prince's sickness and I am worried. He is a good prince and has always tried to do the best for his people. Although I am only a poor soldier and will probably never even meet the prince, I thought I could pray for him. I know that the doctors are very clever

and the royal council is very wise, but I think I may know what is happening to make the prince sick."

"What is that then?" asked the holy man.

"I think that the prince is bewitched," the young samurai replied. "If I can stay just one night with him then I will do everything I can to find out what magic is causing his illness."

The holy man took the samurai straight to the royal council. The members of the council argued between themselves. Some said they should allow the samurai to guard the prince. Others said that it was too great a task for such a young man. At last they decided to allow the young samurai to keep watch.

When the young samurai entered the royal apartment he saw that the prince's bed was in the middle of the room, surrounded by fifty servants. The servants were chatting to each other, trying to keep awake. The young samurai wondered how the prince could sleep through such a noise. But at midnight all fifty servants fell fast asleep.

The young samurai tried to keep his eyes open. He sang songs and pinched himself, but he became more and more sleepy. He realised that if he wanted to stay awake he would have to try extreme methods. He pressed the point of his knife against his thigh. The pain of the knife kept him awake for a time, but eventually he felt his eyes closing once more. He pushed the knife harder against his thigh, and increased the pain and kept himself awake. Only samurai are trained in such methods and it is both foolish and dangerous for anyone else to try.

The young samurai waited and waited until finally the doors to the balcony opened. In came a beautiful woman. It was the demon cat, disguised as Toya. She smiled when she saw the sleeping servants and walked toward the prince's bed.

"Stop," demanded the young samurai, leaping to his feet.

"Who are you?" the demon cat demanded angrily.

"I am Ito Soda, a young samurai," he replied.

"Well, you shouldn't be in here," she said.

"I have sworn to stay awake and guard the prince," argued the samurai.

88

"Ah," said the woman. "And how is the prince tonight?" She walked up to the bed, but when she came close the young samurai raised his sword.

"Come no nearer," warned the samurai, so the false Toya rushed from the prince's room screaming with anger and frustration.

In the morning the fifty servants woke up. They felt very guilty when they realised that the young samurai had managed to stay awake while they were sleeping. The royal council praised Ito Soda for his courage and asked him to watch over the prince again. So for another night the young samurai watched over the sleeping prince. Once again the false Toya came to the prince's bed, but she left without being able to cast her spell over him.

As long as the young samurai was beside his bed, the false Toya kept away and the prince slept peacefully. The prince began to get better. Once he was well enough to speak with the council and the samurai, he called them to his bedroom.

"The woman who called herself Toya must be an evil creature," said the prince. "Ito Soda, you must destroy it, whatever it is."

So that night the young samurai went to the false Toya's room to kill her. Eight other soldiers stood outside in case she tried to escape. The samurai knocked on the door and called out.

"Madam, I have a message for you from the prince."

"What is the message?" the false Toya asked.

"Please open the door and read the letter," replied Ito Soda. But he didn't really have a letter in his hand. Instead, he held his sword.

The door swung open and there stood the false Toya with a sword in her hand too. The false Toya leapt high into the air, attacking Ito Soda with all her strength.

91

They fought, long and hard. The young samurai had to use every skill and trick he had been taught to defeat the false Toya.

Eventually she knew that she was beaten and decided to escape while she could. She threw away her sword, turned back into the demon cat and jumped onto the roof. The eight men waiting outside shot at the animal with arrows, but it moved too fast and raced away into the night. The demon cat headed straight for the hills, back to the cave where it held the real Toya prisoner.

As time passed and nobody came to rescue her, the real Toya grew very unhappy and worried. She thought that everyone had forgotten her and that she would have to spend the rest of her life in the demon cat's cave. However, back at the palace the prince had recovered slowly from his illness and now he was determined to find her.

"I know she is alive somewhere," he told the royal council. "If we find that demon cat's cave, my Toya is sure to be there."

One day, reports reached the palace of a fierce creature that had been seen roaming the hills. The prince sent a small army to find it. They spent weeks in the hills going from village to village and from cave to cave searching for the demon cat. Eventually the army reached the cave where Toya was being held prisoner.

It was dark in the cave and only one soldier dared to go inside. Can you guess who it was? Of course, it was the brave young samurai, Ito Soda. He took out his sword and entered the cave.

There, crouching in the corner, was the demon cat. It rushed at the young samurai and fought him fiercely, but this time there was nowhere for it to run. The young samurai killed the evil creature with his sword.

93

At the back of the cave Ito Soda found Toya hiding. She was tired and hungry but very pleased to see him. She was as beautiful and good as ever and thanked the young samurai for his courage. Ito Soda took Toya back to the palace and the prince cried with joy when he saw her.

The prince married Toya and, since the couple were generous, they thanked everyone who had helped them. They gave Ito Soda a fine horse and a fortune in gold. In time, the young samurai became a famous general, and protected the prince and his family for many years to come.

The Soldier and the Magic Whistle

A soldier marched down the road with a rucksack on his back and a sword at his side. *One two, one two, one two.* At a bend in the road he met an old woman – a witch. She was dressed in black, and her chin and nose were so long that they almost met.

"Good evening, young man," the witch said to the soldier. "What a handsome soldier you are. How would you like to be a rich soldier too?"

"It depends what I must do," the soldier replied, because he knew you should never trust a witch.

"See that big tree beside the road?" asked the witch, pointing to a large oak. "It is hollow. Climb up the trunk and you will see a hole that goes straight through its middle into the ground. Climb down the hole with a rope tied round your waist and I'll pull you up when you call."

"But what must I do inside the tree?" the soldier asked.

"At the base of the tree you will find an underground passage," said the witch. "Along the passage you will see three doors leading in to three separate rooms. In each room there is a dog sitting on a box. Pick up the dog and put it on the ground. Then you can open the box and take out all the money you want."

"What's in it for you?" asked the soldier.

"The money is all yours," said the witch. "All I want is an old whistle you will find in the passage."

"OK," said the soldier. "Give me the rope."

The soldier tied the rope around his waist and climbed up the tree. Sure enough, there was a hole that went straight through the middle of the tree and into the ground. Everything was exactly as the witch had said. He found himself in a passage with three doors. He opened the first door and inside he could see a strange dog with eyes as big as saucers sitting on a box. The soldier stared at the dog and the dog stared back. Then the soldier picked it up, put it on the ground and opened the box. It was filled to the brim with copper coins that he stuffed into his pockets and into his bag.

Then the soldier went to the next room. The dog in the second room had eyes as big as plates. The soldier picked it up and put it on the ground. Inside the box the soldier found hundreds of silver coins, so many, in fact, that he threw out the copper coins and took silver ones instead.

Then he went into the third room. There sat the strangest dog yet. Its eyes were as big as the wheels on a bicycle. The dog's eyes rolled round and round, making the soldier feel a little dizzy. In the third box there was enough gold to buy a castle. The soldier emptied out the silver coins and filled his pockets with gold ones instead.

Then he put the dog back on top of the box and shut the door. He ran back through the passage to the hole and shouted to the old woman outside.

"I'm ready. Pull me up, old woman!"

"Have you got the whistle?" she asked.

"Oops!" said the soldier. "I almost forgot it."
He went back and found an old whistle lying in the passage. Then the witch pulled him up. Soon he stood blinking in the sunshine, his pockets bulging with gold.

"Give me the whistle," demanded the witch.

"Why do you want it so much?" asked the soldier.

"That's none of your business," hissed the witch.

"How do I know you won't use it for mischief?" asked the soldier.

"You've got your money. Now give me the whistle," demanded the witch.

"Tell me what you're going to do with it or I'll cut off your head," threatened the soldier.

"Give me my whistle!" the witch yelled, and she jumped on the soldier, kicking and screaming. Quick as a flash, the soldier drew his sword and cut off her head.

The soldier set off for the nearest town. There he found the best hotel, ordered the biggest room, bought the newest shoes, the finest clothes and ate a meal fit for a king. The soldier had always been poor, so he loved the fact that even the waiters treated him like a gentleman. One of them told him about the king and queen of the land, and their beautiful daughter Princess Olivia.

"How can I meet the princess?" asked the soldier.

"Oh, you can't," said the waiter. "She lives in a castle surrounded by guards. Only the king and queen are allowed in and out."

"Poor princess," sighed the soldier. "Why do they keep her prisoner?"

"Because a fortune-teller once told the king that his daughter would marry a humble soldier," the waiter replied. "The king couldn't stand the idea and locked her up to prevent it. Just between you and me, they do say that the king's a big bully."

The soldier enjoyed his life, spending all his money. He bought a small castle and entertained all his friends. He also gave a lot of money to the poor. Everyone agreed that he was a thoroughly generous man, but he never forgot about the princess.

Alas, nothing lasts forever. Soon all the soldier's money was gone. He had to leave his beautiful home and go to live in a damp attic. There were no waiters, no expensive clothes and none of his friends came to see him.

Eventually the soldier hadn't enough money for candles, so he sat in the dark without any light. It was then that he remembered the whistle. He decided to play a tune to raise his spirits. So he found it, put it to his lips, and blew once. Nothing. The soldier couldn't hear anything at all. Then suddenly, there in front of him appeared the dog with eyes as big as saucers.

"What are your orders, Master?" it asked.

"Hello," said the soldier. "You want orders do you? Could you bring me some money?"

The dog disappeared, but returned instantly, carrying a big bag of copper coins. The soldier was amazed.

Now he realized the true value of the magic whistle – the owner of the whistle was also the master of the three magic dogs. Human ears couldn't hear the sound of the whistle, but the dogs' ears were specially tuned to hear it and obey. The soldier quickly regained his fortune, and went back to live in his elegant house. Soon his friends were visiting again and the town's poor rejoiced at the money he gave away.

Then one night he remembered the beautiful princess who was locked in a castle. He blew on his magic whistle – once, twice. Up popped the dog with eyes as big as plates.

"What are your orders, Master?" the dog asked.

"I want to see Princess Olivia," said the soldier.
The dog set off for the castle. He picked up Princess
Olivia, who was fast asleep, and carried her on his back.
He carried her through a window and swam the castle's
moat. Then he dug a tunnel underground until he was
past the soldiers guarding the castle.

Olivia was the most beautiful woman the soldier had
ever seen and he had to kiss her. The princess, however,
slept on and eventually the dog took her away.

At breakfast the next day, the princess told her parents what a strange dream she had had that night. She explained all about riding on a dog's back and being kissed by a soldier.

"I don't like the sound of that," thought the king. So he ordered a servant to watch the princess all night to find out the truth about her dream.

The soldier was desperate to see the princess again, so the next evening he sent the dog with eyes as big as plates to bring her to him.

When the dog entered the princess's room the servant was waiting. He followed the dog back to the soldier's house. To make sure he would be able to find the house again, he marked the door with a big, chalk 'X'. Then the servant went home to bed.

Near dawn, the dog slipped out of the soldier's house to return the princess to the castle. Luckily, the dog noticed the chalk on the door. Thinking quickly, it drew chalk marks on all the doors in the town.

Early the next morning, the king and queen went with the servant to find the house that the princess had been taken to.

"Here it is," said the king, when they came to the first door with an 'X' on it.

"No, darling, it must be this one," said the queen, pointing to a second door that also had an 'X' on it.

"But all the doors have chalk marks!" they exclaimed. There was chalk on every door in every street. The royal couple realized their search was useless.

However, the queen had an idea. She made a little silk bag and filled it with flour. At night, when the princess was asleep, the queen tied the bag around her daughter's neck. Then she cut a tiny hole in the bag, so that the flour would trickle out onto the ground. That night, the dog came again and carried Princess Olivia on his back. He didn't notice the trail of flour forming behind him all the way from the castle to the soldier's house.

In the morning, the king's guards came to the house and arrested the soldier. They threw him into a dark, damp dungeon full of rats and spiders. The soldier begged to see the king.

"I love your daughter," the soldier confessed.
The king was outraged.

"Hang him!" he demanded.
The guards took the poor soldier back to the dungeon. He was powerless because he had left the magic whistle in his bedroom.

The night before his execution, he hardly slept at all.

In the morning he peered through the bars of his dungeon and watched as people gathered to see him hanged. In the crowd the soldier saw the waiter to whom he had spoken when he first arrived in the town. He called out to him from his dungeon.

"Please, I need your help. Run to my bedroom and bring me my whistle. I will pay you well."
The waiter liked the soldier because he had always left very good tips, so he went to fetch the whistle.

When evening came, the guards took the soldier out to the scaffold, the place where they hang all the criminals. The whole town had come to watch, including the king and queen. When the guards placed the rope around his neck, the soldier asked for one last thing.

"Your Highness, may I play my whistle to cheer my final minutes before I am executed?"

The king and queen thought he was a fool, but let him play the whistle anyway. The soldier blew the whistle once, twice, three times and in a flash all of the dogs appeared – the one with eyes as big as saucers, the one with eyes as big as plates and even the one with eyes as big as bicycle wheels that went round and round.

"What are your orders, master?" the dogs asked.

"Quick," shouted the soldier. "Get me out of this mess!"
And the dogs were very quick. They seized the king's guards and tossed them high into the air so that they landed in a tangled heap on the floor. Then they bounded over to the king's throne. The dog with the eyes as big as bicycle wheels grabbed the king and the queen, and threw them up into the air so they landed on top of the guards.

The people could see how powerful the soldier was and many knew of his generosity.

"You should be our king," they cried. "And you should marry Princess Olivia."

The soldier rushed to the castle to rescue the princess. He married her and she became queen. Their wedding was a great celebration. It lasted a whole week and all the people of the kingdom were invited, rich and poor alike. Place of honour was reserved for the three magic dogs. Throughout the meal they sat in silence and stared at everyone with their big, round eyes.

Hansel and Gretel

In a land far away, a woodcutter and his wife lived with their two children, Hansel and Gretel. Times were very hard. One night, when Hansel and Gretel went to bed they were so hungry that their tummies grumbled loudly. They lay awake, listening to their parents who were arguing in the kitchen.

Their father was a good man, but their mother was cruel and impatient. She paced about the kitchen, banging the pots and pans.

"I've had enough," she hissed. "There is no more food and soon we will all starve."

"Better to starve together," said the woodcutter. "I would give my last crumb to you and the children."

"It's the children who are the problem," said his wife. "Get rid of them and we might just survive."

"B-b-but," their father stammered. "We can't. You don't mean it!"

"The choice is simple," said the children's mother. "It's them or us. I've decided. Tomorrow we shall take them deep into the forest and leave them there. Trust me. You will thank me in the end."

The woodcutter fell silent. He loved his children, but he was afraid of his wife. Hansel and Gretel heard him agree with his wife. They were horrified.

"Oh, Hansel," said Gretel. "We must think of a way to keep ourselves safe."

So that night, when the woodcutter and his wife had gone to bed, Hansel tiptoed outside. It was a clear night and all around the house small, white pebbles shone in the moonlight. He filled his pockets with the pebbles and slipped back to bed.

The next morning their parents woke Hansel and Gretel early. Their mother gave them a loaf of bread to share, and together they all left the house. The woodcutter walked grimly up ahead, while their mother dragged Gretel by the hand. Hansel walked some paces behind.

Hansel's mother soon grew impatient with her son.
  "Get a move on, you lazy child," she said. "Why are you so slow?"
  "I'm waving goodbye to our cat who is sitting on the

cottage roof," Hansel pretended. Really he was dropping the pebbles to make a trail they could follow later.

They walked long and far, deep into the dark wood, until at last they stopped in a small clearing. They were exhausted from walking all day.

"Stay here and sleep," said their mother. "Your father and I will collect some wood to make a fire."

So Hansel and Gretel lay down. They could hear their father chopping wood in the distance so, feeling safe, they fell asleep. When they woke up it was dark and the fire had gone out. They ate the bread that their mother had given them and then walked toward the sound of their father chopping wood. But all they found was a branch creaking in the wind. Their parents were nowhere to be seen.

111

The children had been left all alone.

"Don't worry," said Hansel. They waited until the moon was high in the sky and the pebbles that Hansel had dropped began to shine brightly.
All night long they followed the pebbles home. At last they found themselves on the edge of the forest outside their cottage.

Their mother was shocked to see them. To hide her surprise, she told them off for getting lost. However, the woodcutter was delighted to see them back safely.

The joy at their return was soon forgotten. The family was still poor and there was still no food to eat. Hansel and Gretel lay awake in bed listening, as once again their mother plotted.

"This time we will take the children deeper into the forest," she said. "So deep that they will never find their way home." And once again Hansel and Gretel heard their father agree.

So that night Gretel got out of bed and went outside to gather more pebbles. But her mother had locked the door and she couldn't get out. The children realized they would have to think of something else.

Their mother woke them early the next morning. She gave them some bread and the family strode off. Their father walked up ahead, while their mother dragged Hansel by the hand and Gretel dawdled behind.

"Get a move on you lazy girl," said the mother again. "Why are you so slow?"

"I was just waving goodbye to a dove that is sitting on our roof," Gretel pretended. Really she was breaking her bread and scattering breadcrumbs to make a trail to follow later.

They walked further than they had gone before, on and on through the forest. It was late afternoon when they stopped. Once again their mother told them to lie down and sleep. Exhausted, the children lay down. They tried to stay awake, but soon they were fast asleep. They awoke to discover that their parents had deserted them again.

It was dark and they were cold. Gretel had used all the bread to make the trail to take them home, so they were very hungry too.

"Don't worry," said Gretel. "As soon as the moon rises, we'll find the breadcrumbs and follow them home."

But when the moonlight came they couldn't find the crumbs anywhere. The birds of the forest had eaten every last one. They looked for their cottage, but the forest was too thick, and they just went round and round in circles. For three days they ate berries and fell asleep on the forest floor, until they grew dizzy from hunger.

"We really are lost now," Hansel whispered anxiously. Just then they heard a bird singing. The children saw a white dove high in the treetops. It flew from branch to branch and sang so beautifully that the children decided to follow it.

Through the trees they went and over a small hill. Then they stopped and stared, because in front of them was an amazing house that glistened like an iced cake. When the children looked more closely, they couldn't believe their eyes. The walls of the house were made of gingerbread.

The children were so hungry that they tore out a gingerbread brick and gobbled it up. It was delicious! Next, Gretel tried a piece of the window. It was made of clear butterscotch and melted on her tongue. Hansel tugged at the roof. Instead of straw, the roof was made of marzipan. The gingerbread house was the most amazing, tasty house they had ever seen.

115

The children were so busy eating that they didn't hear the door creak open. Out stepped an old woman. Her face was covered with a black shawl. The children stopped eating and stared. All they could see was a long, hairy chin and bright red eyes.

"Hello, children," the old woman said. Her breath was rotten, but her words were kind. "If you want some food, I have plenty, and somewhere to sleep too. Don't be afraid. I'm an old lady who lives alone, and I mean you no harm."

So Hansel and Gretel went inside, and sat down at a table where the woman brought them more delicious food. Then she took them to a bedroom where there were two soft, clean beds. Hansel and Gretel thanked the old woman and went to bed.

Unfortunately for Hansel and Gretel, there was danger ahead. The old woman chuckled to herself. The children didn't know it yet, but she was a witch, and the gingerbread house was just her trap to capture them. The witch was almost blind, but her sense of taste and smell were as sharp as a knife. More than anything she liked eating children.
She fried them, boiled them and baked them, but best of all the witch liked to make 'children stew'.

At dawn she grabbed Hansel from his bed and locked him in a cage.
"Now I've got you," she cackled. Then she squeezed Hansel's finger. Since the witch could hardly see, this was the only way she could tell how fat Hansel was.

"Not bad," the witch muttered. "I will feed you, fatten you and soon you will be good enough to put in a stew." While Hansel was in the cage, the witch made Gretel work hard. The young girl fetched the wood for the fire, scrubbed the floors and did the washing up. In return, the witch fed her crab shells and cold custard. The witch fed Hansel so much food, however, that he felt sick.

Each day the witch came to check the size of his finger. But Hansel was as a clever boy. When asked for his finger, he held out an old chicken bone instead, so that the blind witch thought he was still skinny.

After a month, the witch's patience gave out.
    "Enough of this waiting!" she said. "Today I want to have my stew."

Gretel was told to fetch wood for a fire, fill a great cauldron with water, and chop a huge pile of vegetables. The witch was going to eat Hansel in a stew.

"Go to the oven, little girl," the witch ordered Gretel. "Pop your head in and tell me if it's hot enough." Now Gretel may have been little, but she was very clever. She knew that the witch planned to bake her in the oven.

"I don't know how to check the oven," said Gretel.

"It's easy," grumbled the witch. "Just open the door and put your head in."

"But I don't know how to open the door," said Gretel.

"You stupid little girl," said the witch, impatient for her dinner. "Can't you do anything? It's easy. I'll show you." The witch went to the oven, opened the door and put her head inside.

"This is how you do it," the witch cackled.

As quick as a flash, Gretel ran and, with all her strength, she pushed the witch head first into the oven. Then she slammed the door shut. The witch let out a terrible scream, but soon she was little more than smoke and ash.

Gretel ran to her brother and unbolted the door of the cage.

"Quick Hansel," she cried. "We must escape from this terrible place. But first I have a secret to tell you. Every day, for weeks, I have cleaned this gingerbread house. I have swept every corner and dusted every drawer. Soon I discovered that the wicked witch must have been robbing and killing people for years, just to steal their treasure. There are boxes of treasure hidden all over the house, filled with beautiful jewels and gold coins."

This time it wasn't bread or pebbles the children filled their pockets with before they entered the forest. They left the witch's house with all the jewels and gold they could carry.

Trying to remember which path to follow, they walked back through the forest. Eventually, they saw the chimney

of their own cottage. Nervously, they knocked at the door, afraid of what their cruel mother would say when she saw that they had found their way home again.
It wasn't their mother who opened the door. Their father stood before them. He looked tired and sad, but his face lit up when he saw Hansel and Gretel standing on the doorstep.

"Children, come in. Your mother has gone away. She was a bad woman, but I was weak to agree to her evil plans. Can you ever forgive me?" he begged.
"Of course. We love you, Father," both the children assured him, and hugged him.

That evening, when they were all gathered around the hearth, they told their father all about their adventures. They told him about the gingerbread house, the witch and her amazing treasure. The woodcutter hugged his children and told them that he would never leave them.

From that day forward they stayed together, rich and prosperous, and the best thing was that Hansel and Gretel were never hungry again.

Thumbelina

Once upon a time there was a woman who desperately wanted a child. She felt so sad and lonely that she went to see a wise, old fairy to ask her advice. The fairy knew just what to do, but it certainly wasn't what the woman had expected.

"Take this magic seed," said the fairy. "Plant it in a flowerpot, water it and see what happens."
The woman took the seed and did exactly as the fairy had told her. She watered the soil and then went to bed.

In the morning she checked the pot and found that the seed had grown into a large, white flower. Its leaves were tightly closed in a bud, but when the woman touched it, the bud went *Pop!* The woman could hardly believe her eyes. The flower opened, and inside lay a tiny, but very beautiful, girl.

She was hardly as big as a thumb, so the woman called her Thumbelina.

The woman loved Thumbelina and tried to make her happy. She put a plate full of water on a table and decorated the edge of the plate with flowers. She floated a tulip leaf on the water, which Thumbelina used as a boat. Thumbelina rowed herself from side to side, with two oars made from the mane of a white horse.

The woman also made the little girl a bed from a walnut shell. On it she placed blue violet petals for a mattress and a rose petal as a quilt. Every night Thumbelina snuggled up in the walnut shell to sleep. However, one night, something terrible happened.

124

While Thumbelina was asleep, a toad crept into her room.

"My, my," said the toad. "This pretty girl would make a perfect wife for my son."

So she picked up Thumbelina and hopped out of the window. She carried Thumbelina to the stream. Her son was on the bank waiting for his mother, because he never did anything without her. He was ugly and warty, and all he could say was "Croak".

To stop Thumbelina from running away, the toad and her son put her on a water lily that grew in the middle of the stream. When Thumbelina woke up she was terrified. To her, the leaf of the water lily was like an island in a huge, swirling sea. There was no escape. The toad and her son were always watching her.

"Tomorrow you must marry my son," the mother toad said. "You will live together in the mud and be happy."

"Croak," said the toad's ugly son. They plopped into the water and swam away.

What was Thumbelina to do? She didn't want to marry a toad, especially one that could only say "Croak". She didn't love him one little bit. So she sat down on the water lily and cried.

The little fishes in the stream heard Thumbelina crying and felt sorry for her. They swam to the bottom of the stream and gnawed at the green stalk of the water-lily leaf until it broke. The leaf floated off downstream, carrying the tiny girl far away, until she was safe from the toad and her son.

As Thumbelina sailed along the stream, a graceful white butterfly fluttered around her. Eventually it settled next to her on the leaf. Thumbelina took the ribbon from her hair, tied one end of it round the butterfly, and fastened the other end to the leaf. When the butterfly flew off it pulled Thumbelina and the leaf towards the bank.

Unfortunately, there were other insects living on the riverbank, and before Thumbelina could climb to safety, a huge beetle flew by. He swooped down, snatched her up in his claws, and flew up into a tree. The beetle took her high into the branches of the tree.

He thought that Thumbelina was very beautiful, and stared at her for hours with his strange, beady eyes.

Eventually some other beetles passed by. When they saw Thumbelina they laughed.

"She's only got two legs," they cried. "She is *soooo* ugly."

Now this confused the beetle. He thought Thumbelina was beautiful, but if his friends said she was ugly then maybe he was wrong. The beetle decided that the easiest thing to do was to get rid of her, so he picked her up again, and flew down and placed her on the forest floor.

All summer long, little Thumbelina lived alone in the forest. She was never idle. She made a bed by weaving blades of grass, and hung it up under a broad cloverleaf to protect her from the rain. She sucked honey from the flowers and drank dew from their leaves. Her only company was the sweet sound of a swallow that sang overhead.

Soon autumn came, and life grew harder. Her grass bed rotted, her cloverleaf roof blew away, and the flowers that she ate from shrivelled and died. Even the swallow that sang to her flew away. Without friends, shelter or food, Thumbelina had a miserable time and nearly froze. She was a delicate girl, and her old clothes were no protection against the cold.

As if things weren't bad enough, when winter arrived it brought snow. When you are a big person, the snow can be fun, but Thumbelina was tiny. Imagine someone throwing pillows at you from the sky. They would knock you to the ground. That was what each snowflake felt like to Thumbelina. It was no wonder she was scared. She wrapped herself up in a dry leaf for warmth, and decided to go and look for shelter.

Through the snow she struggled, until she came across a little house hidden in a cornfield. She sheltered in the doorway and shivered. Luckily the house belonged to a friendly fieldmouse, and when he opened the door and found Thumbelina, he took pity on her.

"You poor little thing," the fieldmouse said. "Come in, and warm yourself by the fire."

128

Thumbelina went inside and found the fieldmouse's friend, who was sitting sipping tea. He was a blind mole, small, black and velvety.

"This is Mole," said the fieldmouse. "He is my good friend. He has a beautiful house that is big and luxurious. Everyone who lives in the cornfield would like to marry Mr. Mole."

The fieldmouse winked at Thumbelina. He showed her to a large, comfortable armchair. They warmed themselves by the fire, eating tea and toast. The fieldmouse asked Thumbelina if she would sing for them, and she was happy to oblige. Her song drifted through the house like sweet perfume. Mole was blind and couldn't see a thing, but he fell in love with her voice instantly.

The fieldmouse was delighted, and let Thumbelina stay in his house. Thumbelina was grateful to the fieldmouse for taking her in, but she feared that he wanted her to marry Mole. Sure enough, a wedding day was set for spring. Thumbelina tried not to think about it. She was sad because she didn't love Mole one little bit.

Every day, throughout the winter, Thumbelina was sent to Mole's house deep underground to sing. To get to Mole's house, Thumbelina had to walk through a long tunnel, and one day she found a dead swallow lying in the middle of the tunnel. The poor bird must have died of the winter cold and fallen in through the tunnel roof. Thumbelina knelt down and stroked the soft feathers on the swallow's head.

"Perhaps this was the bird that sang to me in the summer," she thought. So she wove a large blanket out of hay and spread it over the swallow to keep him warm. Kneeling down once again, she hugged the bird. *Thump, thump!* Thumbelina leapt up in surprise. Could that be the sound of the bird's heart beating? Perhaps he wasn't really dead, only stiff with cold, and the warm blanket had brought him back to life.

131

All winter long, Thumbelina nursed the swallow with love and care. Mr. Mole and the fieldmouse didn't notice how much time she spent in the tunnel between their houses.

When spring came, the swallow was strong enough to fly. Thumbelina broke open the roof of the tunnel and in streamed the beautiful, warm sunshine.

"Thumbelina," said the swallow. "You saved my life. Come with me and I will take you to my home in a beautiful land."

"I can't," cried Thumbelina. "It would break the fieldmouse's heart if I left."

"Then goodbye, and good luck, dear Thumbelina," said the swallow, and off he flew.

Thumbelina didn't want to stay, because she knew it meant that she would have to marry Mole. Soon she would be taken to live in his dark house, deep under the ground.

When the morning of the wedding arrived, Thumbelina stood in the sunshine for the last time.

"Goodbye flowers," she cried. "Goodbye trees. Goodbye bright sun."

Just then, Thumbelina heard a song. It was the swallow.

"Quick, Thumbelina!" he called. "You can't live underground with Mole. You must come with me."

"Yes, take me with you," begged Thumbelina. She climbed on to his back and held on tight.

The swallow soared up into the air and flew far, far away.

They soared over forests, seas
and high mountain peaks
until they flew so high that
Thumbelina's breath froze.
She crept under the swallow's
soft feathers to keep warm.

Eventually they reached a
beautiful land where the sun
shone all day long. Fat purple
grapes hung from vines and
the branches of the trees
dipped low from the weight
of the fruit growing on them.
The air smelled of orange
blossom, and there was music
everywhere, a symphony of
birdsong.

Far below, Thumbelina spotted a blue lake, and beside it stood a dazzling white palace. Lush green vines grew up the palace walls and that was where the swallow and his friends made their nests.

"My home is too high above the ground for you, Thumbelina," said the swallow. "Choose one of the flowers that grow in the palace garden and you can make it your home."
Thumbelina pointed to a beautiful white flower that reminded her of the one in which she was born. The swallow flew down and placed her on one of its broad petals. In the middle of the flower sat a tiny man, not much larger than Thumbelina herself. On his head he wore a golden crown, and on his back were two delicate fairy wings.

"What a handsome man," whispered Thumbelina.
"What a beautiful girl," the little man thought when he saw Thumbelina.
They both fell in love immediately.
"What is your name?" the little man asked.
"Thumbelina," she replied.
He took the gold crown from his head and placed it on hers.
"Thumbelina, will you marry me, and be queen of all the flowers?" he begged.
"Oh, yes please," said Thumbelina.
Then, all the flowers opened, and out of each danced a little man or a little woman. Each of them was carrying a gift for Thumbelina. The best gift of all was a pair of beautiful white wings. Two tiny ladies helped tie the

134

wings on to Thumbelina's shoulders. She flapped her new wings and found that she could fly from flower to flower whenever she wanted.

Thumbelina's travels were over, and she was glad that she had waited for a husband that she loved. On the day she married the King of Flowers, the flower people threw a huge party to celebrate. Thumbelina's favourite part of the day was when her old friend, the swallow, sang her a song. It was about how beautiful and kind Thumbelina was, and how she was now the Queen of Flowers.

The Wild Swans

Far away, in a land of endless summers, lived a king who had eleven sons and one daughter. The daughter's name was Eliza, but her father and brothers all called her Ellie, which she preferred.

At school, the children wore gold stars on their caps to show that they were royal children. They all wrote with diamond pencils and read from beautiful picture books that were worth their weight in gold. They were happy, fortunate children, loved and well cared for.
But things were about to change.

137

One day their mother died. Their father, the king, was heartbroken and became very lonely. In what seemed like no time at all, however, he met and married a wicked woman, who became queen.

The new queen was very jealous of Ellie, whom everybody loved. She was so jealous that she sent Ellie away to live with a poor family in a nearby forest. The queen also made up lies about Ellie and the princes, so that the king would not love them any more.

One day, the queen went into the princes' bedroom.
"Get out of here!" she cried, and chanted a terrible spell.
"Fly away, fly away, fly away.
Become little silent birds, I pray."

But the princes were
strong young men, and the
magic could only turn them into
eleven beautiful, wild swans. With a
screech and a yell, they flew out of the
windows of the palace and into the forest beyond.

They passed the cottage where Ellie was staying, but she
lay asleep in her room. They screeched as loud as they
could, but no one heard them. At last they flew over the
sea to another land. They found a cave on a hillside and
settled down to a new life.

139

As the weeks turned into years, Ellie grew into a beautiful young woman. She was very lonely. She missed her brothers and had no friends to talk to.

On her sixteenth birthday, Ellie returned to the palace, but when the queen saw how beautiful Ellie was, she spat with envy. She went to her box of magic and took out three toads. She knew a spell that could make even the brightest and most beautiful person become stupid and ugly.

Early the next morning, the queen went into Ellie's bathroom. She kissed each of the toads in turn.

"Sit on Ellie's hair so that she becomes as stupid as you," she said to the first toad. "Sit on her forehead so that she becomes as ugly as you are," she said to the second toad. "Sit on Ellie's heart so that she has evil thoughts," she said to the third. Then she put all the toads into the bath. The water turned a slimy green colour immediately.

The queen woke Ellie and helped her to get undressed and into the bath. One of the toads hopped on to Ellie's hair, a second on to her forehead, and a third on her breast, but the girl did not seem to notice them. You see, Ellie was too good for the queen's witchcraft to work, and when she got out of the bath there were three beautiful red poppies in place of the toads.

The wicked queen was so angry that she dragged Ellie into the garden and rubbed her face with mud, tangled her beautiful hair and smeared her all over with oil. Soon it was impossible to recognize the beautiful Ellie. When the king, her father, saw her, he was shocked.

"This filthy creature cannot be my daughter," he said.

Poor Ellie wept and longed for her eleven brothers, wherever they were. As fast as her legs would carry her, she ran away from the palace. For days she crossed fields and moors until at last she came to a forest. She thought she might find her brothers there, but the forest was thick and deep. Before long Ellie was lost.

Darkness fell and Ellie lay down on some moss and wept. Eventually she fell asleep, dreaming of her brothers.

141

The next day, Ellie journeyed on until she heard water rippling along a stream into a lake with golden sands. The lake was clear and still, and when Ellie bent her head over it she saw her own face and hair. She realized then that she was still filthy, so she undressed and washed in the fresh water, then dressed herself again and braided her long hair.

She felt much better now and wandered further into the forest. On her way, she met a kind old woman, who gave her some strawberries to eat.

"Kind old woman, have you seen my brothers?" Ellie asked. "They are eleven handsome princes and would have ridden through the forest on eleven fine horses."

"No, my dear," replied the old woman. "But yesterday, I saw eleven wild swans on the seashore near here."

Ellie thanked her and followed the river until it widened to the sea. She stepped out on to a pebble beach that stretched far into the distance. Just then, she saw eleven white swan feathers lying on the smooth pebbles of the shore. She gathered them up and, with the feathers in her hand, she sat on the beach, looking out to sea. Ellie thought the sea was beautiful. When the wind blew, the waves became as tall as towers, with icy white tips. When the wind slept, the sea became so calm and creamy, it was like an ocean of fresh milk. When the sun was setting, the clouds glowed red so that the waves looked like the petals of a rose.

As Ellie looked out at the sea, she saw eleven white swans flying towards the land. They flew in a line, one behind the other, like a long white ribbon.

Ellie hid behind some bushes. The swans landed and flapped their great, white wings. As soon as the sunset disappeared, the feathers of the swans fell off and they turned into her brothers, the eleven princes.

Ellie recognized them immediately and sprang into their arms. The princes were overjoyed to see their little sister again. They laughed, and wept, and hugged, and talked about their adventures.

"By day, we are wild swans," the eldest prince explained. "But as the sun sets, we turn back into humans again. That means we must always be near land before sunset or we will drown in the sea. We live far away from here, over the ocean, a journey of two days. There is nothing but a little rock rising out of the sea between here and there. In the night, when we are human, we have to stand on the rock. Sometimes it's dangerous and the waves crash over us, but once a year we make the journey. We fly over the palace and visit the place where our mother lies buried."

Ellie and her brothers talked long into the night. When the sun rose next morning, the princes changed back into swans, and flew away over the land. Only the youngest remained to keep his sister company.
Towards evening, the rest of Ellie's brothers came back, and as the sun went down they turned back into human beings again.

144

"Tomorrow we must return to our home," the eldest brother said. "We shall not be back for a year, but we can't leave you here by yourself. Perhaps we could carry you across the sea."

"Yes, please," begged Ellie. "Take me with you!"

So they spent the whole night weaving a net with willow branches and rushes. When it was finished, Ellie sat in it. The sun rose and, one by one, as the rays of the sun touched their bodies, the brothers became wild swans once again. They picked up the net with their beaks and flew out to sea. Soon they were far from the land, and Ellie looked over the edge. She was travelling high in the clouds and could barely see the waves on the sea.

The swans were slower than usual, because of the extra weight that they carried. As the evening approached, Ellie began to worry, because the little rock in the ocean was still nowhere to be seen. When the sun set, the swans would be turned to men again, and they would all fall into the sea. The weather was stormy, and from a huge, black cloud she saw brilliant streaks of lightning burst across the sky.

Ellie's heart raced as the sun sank to the edge of the sea and the swans darted down. She thought they were falling, but they flew on. It was raining now. Cold drops lashed her face, but at last she caught sight of the rock. They swooped down and landed, just as the sun disappeared into the sea.

Instead of swans, Ellie saw her brothers standing around her. They linked their arms together to keep her safe. The sea crashed against the rock and covered them with spray. They all sang to keep their spirits up. At sunrise, her brothers changed back into swans and they flew on, with Ellie in the net.

At last, Ellie spied the land to which they were heading, with its mountains, forests, towns and palaces. The swans flew to the large cave in the woods where they had made their home.
Ellie lived happily with her brothers, but more than anything she wanted to find a way to free them from their spell. In her dreams a fairy appeared.
  "You must knit your brothers eleven coats made out of stinging nettles," explained the fairy. "You will find

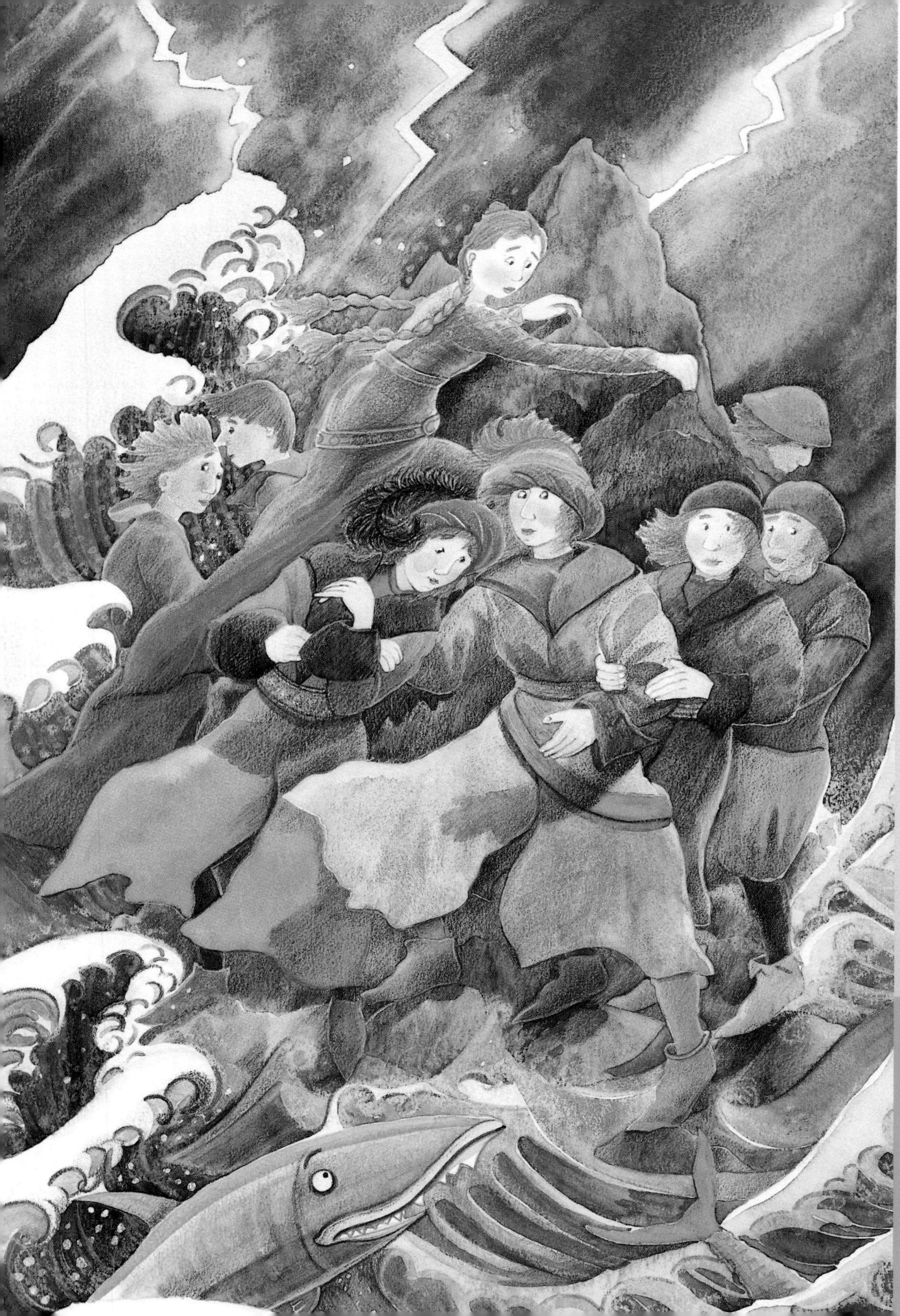

nettles growing around the cave, but if you need more, you can only use nettles that grow in a churchyard. Gather the nettles with your bare hands and crush them with your bare feet. Use them to make thread and use that thread to make eleven coats with long sleeves. If you throw these coats over the eleven swans, the spell will be broken. Remember that, from the moment you start your task, you must not speak. If you say anything at all, your brothers will die. Ellie, you must be brave."
The fairy disappeared and Ellie woke up.

When morning came, Ellie went outside and, sure enough, she found stinging nettles growing near the mouth of the cave. With her bare hands, she picked as many of the nettles as she could find. They burnt and blistered her delicate fingers. She bruised her bare feet crushing the nettles, but she was determined to free her brothers. Next, she made the nettles into thread. At sunset, when her brothers returned, Ellie did not speak to them. She remained silent even though they asked her why she wouldn't speak.

The brothers were worried that Ellie's silence was caused by some new magic, but when they saw her blistered hands they understood that she was making something for them. The youngest brother wept, and as his tears fell on Ellie's blisters, the wounds magically healed straightaway.

Ellie worked all night and all the next day. She finished the first coat and began the second. The next morning, she heard a hunter blowing a horn. Her brothers were not there and the noise was terrifying. The horn became louder, dogs barked and Ellie fled into the cave. She quickly tied her nettles into a bundle and sat on them.

Suddenly, the cave was full of dogs and hunters. The most handsome man among them was the king of the country that Ellie and her brothers had come to. He approached Ellie. He had never seen such a beautiful girl.

"How did you come here?" he asked. But Ellie shook her head. If she spoke her brothers would die.

"Come with me," he said. "If you are as good as you are beautiful, I will marry you."

He lifted her up onto his horse, but Ellie cried because she knew she would not be able to finish the coats.

"I wish only for your happiness," the king promised.

Then he galloped away over the fields and mountains to the castle where he lived. Ellie was taken to a luxurious room and was dressed in silk. She looked so beautiful in her silk gown that everyone at court bowed down when they saw her. Everyone, that is, except the chancellor. He was a cunning man. He was jealous of the fuss everyone was making of Ellie. He wanted to turn the king against her.

"She's a witch, Your Majesty," the chancellor claimed, but the king would not listen to him. He knew the chancellor was a spiteful man.
Ellie was treated very well, but she didn't smile once. Then one day, the king showed her a small room where he had put the bundle of nettles. On the wall hung the coat she had made.

"Here is your work," said the king. "I hope it is what you wanted and that it will make you smile."

Ellie was delighted. She smiled for the first time and kissed the king's hand. The king hugged Ellie tightly.

The kind, handsome king had done everything to make her happy. In her eyes he could see that she loved him, even though she couldn't speak and tell him. Soon, they were married and all the people rejoiced at their new queen.

Every night Ellie left the king and crept away into the small room. She quickly made one coat after another but, by the time she began the seventh, she found she had run out of nettles. She remembered what the fairy had said and decided she would have to find a churchyard and pick the nettles growing there.

One night, she crept out into the moonlight and went through the streets of the town until she reached a churchyard. There were ghosts hovering above the tombstones that looked so horrible, Ellie thought about turning back. However, she was a brave young girl, and she walked past them. The ghosts screamed and tried to frighten her, but ignoring them, she gathered the nettles and took them home to the castle.

Everything had gone well except for one thing – the chancellor had followed Ellie that night. He saw her in the churchyard and told the king what he had seen, but the king would not believe him.

"Ellie's a witch," said the chancellor.

"Don't be silly," scolded the king. "Ellie is innocent." But he began to worry, and wondered what Ellie was doing when she got up in the night to go to her workroom.

Ellie only had one goal, to finish the nettle coats for her brothers. With just one more coat to make she ran out of nettles once again. She would have to return to the churchyard and collect more. Ellie left the castle to gather the precious nettles, but this time both the chancellor and the king followed her.

They saw her vanish into the churchyard. They saw the ghosts who screamed so loud that the earth shook. The king turned back, because he couldn't bear to think Ellie was a witch. He went home to the palace and, after much thought, he ordered that Ellie should be put to death by fire – the usual punishment for witches.

Ellie was led to a dark, dreary cell with iron bars. Instead of her luxurious room and fine dresses, the guards gave her the coats she had been making as a quilt. For a pillow they gave her the bundle of nettles she had gathered in the churchyard. They thought that they were punishing her, but Ellie was delighted. She had only one more coat to make and only one night left to do it. Without even stopping to eat, she started work.

The king went to speak to Ellie, but she was so desperate to finish the coats that she chased him away. He ran out of her cell, fearing she was mad. Ellie only had a few hours to finish, so she carried on her work.

By morning, a huge crowd had gathered to see Ellie's execution. She was dressed in a sack and placed on a cart driven by an old horse. Even on the way to the fire she didn't stop working. The mob jeered at her.

"Burn the witch," they screamed, but still Ellie carried on trying to finish the eleventh coat.

Then the crowd rushed at Ellie and grabbed her, but at that moment eleven wild swans flew down and landed beside Ellie. They flapped their large wings. The crowd was scared and backed away.

154

As quickly as she could, Ellie threw the eleven coats over the swans, and immediately they became eleven handsome princes. Everyone gasped in amazement. Sadly, Ellie had not been able to finish the sleeve of the last coat, so the youngest prince still had a swan's wing, instead of an arm.

155

"Now I can speak," Ellie cried, her first words in months. "I am innocent." And she told the people the sad story of her brothers. When the people realized what had happened they begged her to forgive them, but Ellie was exhausted and fainted into the arms of her brothers.

156

At that moment the fire, that had been lit to burn Ellie, began to splutter and spit. Out flew a flaming branch. Where the branch landed on the floor, a hedge began to grow. In seconds, the hedge was covered with roses. The king plucked the brightest rose, which had the strongest scent, and tucked it in Ellie's hair.

Ellie woke up. As if by magic, all the bells in the kingdom began to ring all by themselves, and birds flew overhead and sang along. The people picked up Ellie, their queen, and carried her on their shoulders back to the castle where she belonged.

East of the Sun, West of the Moon

Once upon a time, there was a family – a mother, a father and ten children. They all lived together in a little cottage, but they were so poor that they often went to bed hungry.

One stormy evening, it was raining so heavily and blowing so hard that the walls of the cottage shook. All the children were huddled together by the fireside. Suddenly someone rapped three times on the window. The father went out to see who it was and was amazed to find a big white bear standing outside the cottage door.

"Good evening," said the white bear.

"Good evening," said the father.

"If you give me your daughter, Kate, I will make you a rich man," said the white bear.

"How do you know Kate?" the man asked.

"Everyone has heard about Kate," the bear replied.

It was true. All of the children who lived in the house were kind, good and pretty, but Kate was the most beautiful and wise. Kate was very special, but her father had to consider the whole family, and he found the white bear's offer very tempting.

"I must ask my daughter," the man told the white bear. So while the white bear waited outside, the man told his family about the offer.

"Are you crazy?" Kate said. "I don't want to live with a big bear."

However, Kate's father told the white bear that he would have an answer for him if he returned in a week's time. During those seven days, the whole family begged Kate to change her mind.

"It's the best for everyone," said her sisters.

"Think of everything we could buy!" said her brothers. Eventually, Kate gave in, and agreed to go away with the white bear.

Exactly one week later, he came back to fetch Kate.

Reluctantly, she climbed up on to his shoulders.

"Are you afraid?" the bear asked.

"No," replied Kate, who was brave as well as good.

"Hold on tight to my fur," the white bear said, and off they set.

The white bear ran all night, until at last they reached a great mountain. He walked up to a huge rock, knocked three times, and the rock swung open like a door. Inside was a huge cave, and in the cave was a fantastic castle with rooms that shone with gold and silver. Within the castle was a vast hall with a table filled with delicious food.

The white bear gave Kate a silver bell.

"Whenever you need anything, all you have to do is ring the bell," he told her. "Whatever you want will appear instantly."

Then the white bear vanished. Kate sat down at the table and ate until her tummy was bursting. Feeling very sleepy after her day of adventure, Kate decided that she would like to go to bed. So she rang the bell and in a flash she found herself in a bedroom beside a ready-made bed, with pillows of silk and curtains fringed with gold. She climbed into the bed and tried to sleep.

However, the moment she turned out the light, a young man came into her room and lay down beside her in the bed. It was so dark that Kate couldn't even see him, but she was used to sleeping in a full bed with all her brothers and sisters, so she quickly fell fast asleep.

What she didn't know was that the young man was actually the white bear. Long before, a wicked troll-hag had cast a spell on a handsome prince, forcing him to look like a white bear during the day. Every night, the white bear turned back into the prince.

The next morning, the prince slipped out of Kate's room. Every night he returned, until Kate was very used to his visits. Every day Kate wandered around the castle and at night she slept next to the prince. The castle was packed with beautiful things, but before long she grew sad and lonely. When the white bear asked her why she was so unhappy, Kate told him.
"I want to see my family again."
"I will only agree to the visit on one condition," offered the white bear. "You must promise never to talk to your mother alone when there are no other people in the room. If you do, you will bring great misery to both of us."

161

The next morning, the white bear and Kate set off. They left the castle and the mountain cave behind them, and headed towards the cottage where Kate's family lived. When they were outside the cottage, the bear reminded her of her promise.

"I won't speak to my mother alone," Kate promised.

The family was rich now and when they saw Kate, they had a party to celebrate. Her brothers and sisters showed her all their new toys and they had a huge lunch. Then Kate's mother asked her to come into the kitchen, so they could talk to each other alone. It was just as the white bear had warned.

"But Mother," Kate said. "We can talk here with everyone else around."

Her mother persuaded her to go into the kitchen, however, and eventually Kate told her mother the whole story. She described how every night a young man lay down beside her when the lights were out. She never saw him because he always went away before it grew light in the morning.

"Oh!" cried the mother, horrified. "He's probably a troll. Here, take a candle and hide it in your nightdress. When the young man comes at night, light the candle and look at him when he is asleep, but be very careful not to let any wax drip on him."

Kate took the candle and hid it in her dress. The bear returned and as they were travelling back to the castle, he asked Kate if she had spoken to her mother alone.

"Of course not. I gave you my word," she lied.

By the time they reached the castle, Kate was feeling very guilty for her lies. She couldn't face the bear. She told him she was tired and went straight to her bedroom. Kate climbed into the bed and settled down to sleep. Soon, the young man came and lay down beside her. Quick as a flash, she pulled out the candle and lit it so she could see him. Kate could hardly believe her eyes. He was certainly no troll. He was the handsomest prince she had ever seen. She fell in love with him instantly. She bent to kiss him, but as she leaned forward, three drops of wax dripped on to his shirt and he woke up.

"What have you done?" he cried. "Was this your mother's plan? I begged you not to speak to your mother, and now you have brought misery on both of us.

An evil troll-hag has bewitched me so that I am a white bear by day and a man by night. In just one year's time the spell would have run out and I would have been free. But now it is too late. I must go to the castle where the troll-hag lives with her daughter, a troll princess with a nose like a swordfish. It is this princess that I must marry now."

Kate wept and begged him to take her with him.
    "I'm sorry, my love, but I must go on my own," he said.
    "Tell me the way and I will follow you," Kate urged him.
    "The castle lies east of the sun and west of the moon, but you will never find it," the prince said sadly.
Kate woke in the morning to find both the prince and the castle gone. Instead, she lay in the middle of a thick, dark wood.

165

Bravely, Kate set off to find the prince. She walked for days until at last she came across an old woman sitting on the ground with a golden apple.

"Hello," said Kate. "Do you know the way to the castle where a prince lives with a wicked troll-hag? The castle lies east of the sun and west of the moon."

"I'm afraid I can't tell you where to find the prince or the castle," said the old woman. "But I will lend you my horse and my golden apple. Then you can ride to another old woman who lives not far from here. She might be able to help you. When you get there, just tell the horse to come home again, but you may take the golden apple with you."

So Kate rode until she came to an old woman who was combing her hair with a golden comb.

"Do you know how I can find the way to the castle that lies east of the sun and west of the moon?" Kate asked the old woman.

"I'm afraid not," said the old woman. "But there's another old woman nearby. She's the oldest old woman around – she is absolutely ancient – and she might know. Borrow my horse and my comb. When you get there just tell the horse to go home, but you can take the golden comb with you."

Kate rode on again, and after a very long time she came across an ancient woman, who sat spinning at a golden spinning wheel.

"Hello," said Kate. "Do you know the way to the castle east of the sun and west of the moon?"

"I'm afraid I don't," replied the ancient woman. "I'll bet it takes a long time to get there, if you get there at all. I'll lend you my horse so that you can go to the East Wind. Perhaps he knows where the castle is. When you get there just tell the horse to go home again. You may take the golden spinning wheel with you."

Kate rode for many days before she came to the house of the East Wind.

"Well," the East Wind blew. "I have heard of the prince and of the castle, but I do not know where they are. I've never blown that far myself. If you like I will take you to my brother, the West Wind. He may know, because he's much stronger than I am. Sit on my back and I'll carry you there."

So Kate sat on the East Wind's back and they sped along. But when they got there, the West Wind didn't know where the castle was either.

"No," the West Wind said. "I've never blown that far, but I can take you to the South Wind. He's much stronger than either of us, and he's been all over the place. Sit on my back, and then I will carry you to him."

Kate travelled to the South Wind, who listened to her story about the prince, but he couldn't help.

"I have wandered about a great deal in my time, and in all kinds of places, but I have never blown as far as that. I will take you to my brother, the North Wind.

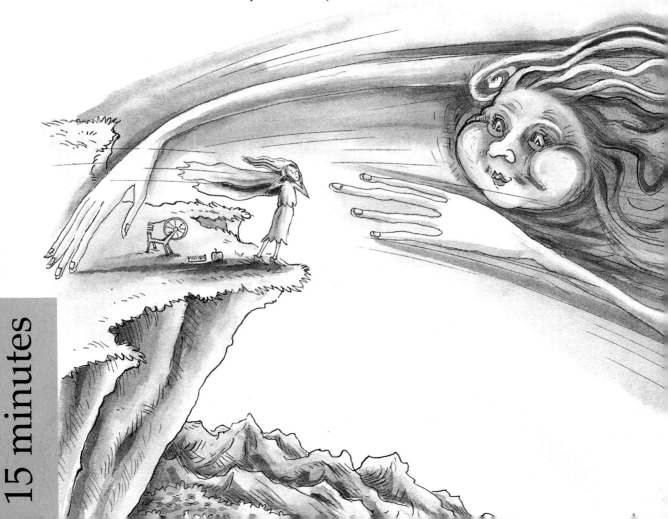

He's the oldest and strongest of all of us. If he does not know where the castle is, then no one does."

Kate sat on the South Wind's back and sped to where the North Wind lived. The North Wind was so wild and frantic that they could feel cold blasts from miles away.
  "What do you want?" the North Wind roared.
  "This is Kate. She is the girl who wants to marry the prince who lives with a troll-hag in the castle which lies east of the sun and west of the moon," explained the South Wind. "She wants to know if you have ever been there and if you can tell her the way."

The North Wind thought for a moment.
  "Yes," he said at last. "I know where the castle is. I once blew an oak leaf there, but I was so tired that it took me days to blow back again."
  Kate was disappointed, but the North Wind was feeling helpful that day.
    "If you've got to get there, and you don't mind going with me..." started the North Wind.
    "I must go there," said Kate. "And I won't be scared, no matter how fast you go."

The North Wind blew himself up, bigger and stronger than all his brothers, until he was ten miles high. Away they went, Kate riding on the North Wind's back.

169

Down below them a storm raged. Over the land, forests and houses fell down. Over the sea, hundreds of ships were being tossed on the waves. On they went, all the way to the end of the world. Gradually the North Wind grew tired. He was so exhausted that he sank lower and lower, until Kate's heels splashed in the waves of the sea.

"Are you afraid Kate?" asked the North Wind.
"No," she said, and it was true.

They were not very far from land now and there was just enough strength left in the North Wind to throw Kate on to the shore. She landed just beneath the windows of the castle, which lay east of the sun and west of the moon.

Not knowing what to do next, Kate sat down by the castle walls and began to play with the golden apple. Looking down from a window was the troll princess with a nose like a swordfish. She was supposed to be marrying Kate's prince.

171

"How much do you want for that golden apple?" the princess asked.

"It's not for sale," answered Kate.

"But I want it," said the princess grumpily.

"You can only have it if I can visit the prince," said Kate.

"OK," replied the princess.

Unfortunately, the troll princess was very cunning and gave the prince a sleeping potion before allowing Kate to visit him. She took the golden apple and let Kate into the castle. But when Kate arrived at the prince's room he was fast asleep. Kate called to him and cried out his name, but she could not wake him. In the morning, the princess chased Kate out of the castle.

Once again, Kate sat under the castle windows and began to comb her hair with the golden comb. The princess looked down again, and wanted to buy the comb.

"It isn't for sale, but I will give it to you if I am allowed to visit the prince again tonight," said Kate firmly.
But when she went up to the prince's room he was asleep again. She shouted and shook him, but still he slept on.

When daylight came, the troll princess came into the bedroom and once more drove Kate away. That day Kate sat under the castle windows and span with her golden spinning wheel. The princess saw the spinning wheel and wanted it. She opened the window and asked Kate if she could buy it. Kate said the same as before, that it was not for sale, but that she would exchange it for one night with the prince.

"Alright," said the princess, "I can arrange that."
In the palace, however, some servants had been working in the room next to the prince's. They told him that the previous two nights they had heard a girl trying to wake him up. So that evening, when the troll princess came into his room with a mug of hot milk full of sleeping potion, the prince pretended to drink it, but threw it away instead.

When Kate arrived, the prince was awake. They hugged each other and she told him all about her adventures.
"You have come just in time, Kate," admitted the prince. "Tomorrow I have to marry the troll princess!" They thought and thought until at last the prince came up with a plan.

15 minutes

"I'll say that I will only marry the woman who can wash the wax out of my nightshirt," the prince explained. "The princess will try, because she doesn't know that it is impossible for a troll to wash the wax out. You're the only one who can do it and you're the only one I want to marry!"

The wedding day arrived, and the prince went to see the princess with a nose like a swordfish, who was sitting

with her troll-hag mother. Her mother, who had a nose like an elephant, was the one who had put the spell on the prince, which changed him into a white bear.

"I have a shirt that I want to wear for the wedding," the prince announced. "But three drops of wax have fallen on it. I will only marry the woman who is able to wash these three drops out."

"Simple," said the princess. She snatched the shirt and began to wash it, but the more she washed, the larger the spots grew.

"Give it to me," demanded her mother. "You can't wash at all." She snatched the shirt, and began to wash it. The more she scrubbed, the larger and blacker the spots grew. All the trolls in the castle came to wash the shirt, but the more they did the worse the spots grew. In the end the shirt looked like it had been worn by a piglet that had been playing in mud.

"Come in Kate!" cried the prince. Kate came in and the prince handed her the shirt. She dipped it in water and, as if by magic, it came out as white as snow.

"Kate, I must marry you," said the prince, delighted.

Then the troll-hag flew into such a rage that she burst. Her daughter burst as well. Soon there were trolls bursting all over the place.

Soon, only Kate and the prince remained. They decided they wanted a fresh start far away, where the walls weren't covered in burst trolls. The prince married Kate and they were very happy, but neither of them ever returned to the castle that lay east of the sun and west of the moon.

Acknowledgements

The publisher would like to thank the following artists for illustrating the stories listed:

The Ugly Duckling, The Fox and the Grapes, The Wolf and the Seven Little Kids, The Twelve Dancing Princesses, Thumbelina
© 2002 by Caroline Anstey

The Emperor with Goat's Ears, The Emperor's New Clothes, The Young Samurai, The Wild Swans
© 2002 by Penny Ives

The Pied Piper of Hamelin, Jack and the Beanstalk, Goldilocks and the Three Bears, The Elves and the Shoemaker, Rumpelstiltskin, Hansel and Gretel
© 2002 by Robin Lawrie

The Three Little Pigs, The Hare and the Tortoise, The Billy Goats Gruff, The Tiger, the Old Man and the Jackal, The Soldier and the Magic Whistle, East of the Sun, West of the Moon
© 2002 by Martin Ursell